Viking's Sacrifice

by

Penny Best

Cover Art by *Lisa Dawn MacDonald*

The Wild Rose Press, Inc.
PO Box 708
Adams Basin, NY 14410-0708
Visit us at www.thewildrosepress.com

Publishing History
First Edition, 2025
Trade Paperback ISBN 978-1-5092-6271-7
Digital ISBN 978-1-5092-6272-4

Published in the United States of America

Dedication

For Victoria

Chapter One

Violent Betrayal

The wash of waves cleared the blood and vomit from her tired fingers as she clung to the nearest rope. Each dive of the vessel sank her despair lower. The other pitiful slaves aboard the Norse longship cried, too. At least she was one of the few hunched under the skin tied over the hull.

One brute edged forward into the small space and looped a rope around her waist. He grunted, yanked tight on the knot, and tied her to the boat. He smelled like a wet goat, possibly a seasoned buck. She retched and clung to the pelt draped over his big shoulders. He heaved her off, stood tall in the keel, and roared something in their foul language. Suddenly, a cascade of water engulfed him, and he was gone.

Thunder boomed overhead, and flashes lit the vicious bearded faces. Open-mouthed with orders, prayers, or worry, they ignored the plight of the stolen bodies around them. Many of her fellow prisoners jumped or allowed themselves to be taken by the sea. She closed her eyes and whispered to her ancestors, urging them to drown them all quickly. Feeble begging to her own Celt gods was of no use. A chieftain father sold her for a foolhardy peace and some stolen gold. She wept again for a mother she never knew and cursed a disinterested father for selling her to these savages.

The relentless swelling monster under them did not relent. All night the storm raged. *These sailors had no control over their fate either. They were all in the same danger.* Sonas laughed uncontrollably until a fist thumped hard across her jaw. Her lip bled.

When she saw the light under the covering, the thwacks on the wood beneath her stopped. There was almost a rhythm to the rocking motion then. But she could not stop shivering. She stared with all her energy at any trace of hope in the whitening sky. Between the rips in the covering, clouds came into view more often. She couldn't feel her sodden feet at all and the chain between them left large welts around her ankles. Her waist was numb, and her hips ached. Some way or another, every part of her body sustained damage. Even her eyes and lips stung from the salt caked there. The deep blisters on her fingers popped and bled in the biting cold air.

Her cries alerted a goat-scented man who loosed her tethering. She neither looked nor thanked him for the release. She smoothed the long hair plaits back from her wet skin and sobbed in self-pity.

She missed the fresh water but clutched the passing beaker on the second passing. She could only gulp three glorious mouthfuls before it disappeared. Thirstier, she opened her mouth to the lightning showers and saw others do the same. The shock of a rogue wave mired the cool relief. Finally the seas eased, and she slumbered from sheer exhaustion.

Sonas awoke to a calm boat and the warmth of the sun. She squinted past the Norsemen gathering to go ashore. She gave gratitude to the rays beyond them. But a foot smacked off her side again and the words meant nothing. She lay there in the glow of the tiny orb and smiled.

The man's rage consumed him. He bent down, and with his immense strength, yanked her upright. He called out, and she lost her balance. Feet crippled under her and a clump of her hair gave way. She fell winded and rolled in agony, unable to avoid the next assault. She shielded her head with heavy arms and screamed.

She could not hear herself, but he stopped the beating. Sonas swallowed a gulp of blood and pain, as she was scooped up and thrown over the shoulder of another savage.

The different brute was angry and yelling. His voice reverberated through him as he clambered them both to solid ground. His hold changed and, with what strength she had, clung to his damp clothes as his arms slid under her failing legs. With a tight, reassuring grasp, he held her and urged her to cling tighter lest she fall farther. He marched through the welcoming throngs and shouted in better tones. He sounded happy to be alive. Legs and bodies passed, and he strode on with Sonas' face against his neck. She breathed against his skin and wondered if she bit downward what would become of her.

His cheek rested against hers and he murmured something soft. His face brushed hers and the bristles of his beard rasped her cheek. He said the same thing again and repeated the words slowly a few times, getting softer still. There was no harshness left between them by the time he attempted to set her upright.

Sonas' curled toes splayed as they met the cold ground. Shakily, she stood hunched over. There was a warmth to her right.

A fire?

She glanced from under her matted hair and saw the sparking logs in a long pit. Her mouth watered at the aroma of cooking meat, and her rescuer's body left her exposed. Alone, she steadied her wobbling legs on the straw floor and stood taller. She reached out for something, for him perhaps, but there were only eyes and laughter.

"This is the stupid chief's daughter. She is called Sonas," a voice said, and she understood those words. With relief, she peered into the half darkness of a large, crowded space. But then, she heard "And her fate is in the hands of the gods."

Chapter Two

Conflict Inside

Ultan sat and watched the woman he had carried from the longship. *Frail. Bleeding. Thin. Filthy. Taking her had been a mistake.*

Shaking his head, Ultan ran a hand over his beard and down the long dark braid hanging over his shoulder. He was as wet through and as cold as the stranger looked.

Was she his slave? Or a sacrifice?

She sank to her knees before the fire pit, and he almost rose to help her again. People would mock his softness. But they talked and hugged. They were glad to be alive. He was, too. Then stories started. As usual, Ultan the Fearless told the tallest tales and laughed the longest. *He liked his home…his father's house. The place smelled the same…was the same.*

His gaze sought the injured woman. She glared through him as if he wasn't a man. She had none of their words, and her vicious eyes peered through her flame-colored hair.

On raids, he never paid heed to the Celtic women. But he'd bartered for the wench. Why?

She had been clean then, in a light-colored dress, her hair loose across her shoulders, her smile broad and she had good teeth. She was healthy for breeding, and nice for a man's bed. Then, he learned she was a chieftain's daughter. A high-born woman who might be good for a sacrifice at Uppsala. He stood forward to win those breasts, legs, and shapely rump. If he wanted to hump, he had a wife and other willing women. Yet he was the one to barter for an innocent, young woman...*because he found her beautiful.*

Guilt rarely gripped Ultan. But she was...*vulnerable now*...He bent the truth. As the leader of a marauding clan, Ultan the Fearless had no right to make big promises to a foolish Irish chieftain. Ultan's fleet was small. There were only five ships left at most, and the true rulers were the ones in Daneland, who were more powerful and farther up the coast. He was not a jarl. But Odin would help him. The drunk Irish chieftain knew no better, and Ultan smirked again, thinking of the low price he had paid for the man's only daughter.

Ultan looked at the one they called Sonas, and the fire leaped across piercing eyes full of tears. She was angry, afraid, and avenging and spoke to him without any voice. She was trouble.

His cock hardened.

What had he done? To her? To his soul?

Ultan's father, Arden, slapped his back and beckoned for him to sit. There was much to do before Ultan took his men to his fortress. He did not want to linger, but the celebrations were high. As they should be. The singing began, and Ultan loved to sing. He drank a lot, ate more of the greasy meat, and wiped dirty hands across his jaws and chest. He hugged the woman he called "Mother," kissed his cousins, and fell onto a bench. Hours passed, and he searched the longhouse for her.

Where was she? The doors had guards. She could

not escape. Someone would have fed her by now. She was by the fire...Yet she was not there.

Ultan stood, swayed, and peered through his family and friends. "Sonas?" he bellowed in the finish. "Sonas? Did someone give the slaves food and ale?" There was a murmuring of agreement it should be done.

"Answer me! Sonas?" Ultan called again. And then, down to the right, he saw the creature crawling out from the shadows. "Come," he ordered.

People talked, and the singing continued. Ultan filled his cup and grabbed a bite of bread. Beckoning to the woman, he smiled. *What was she doing just standing there like a fool? Did she not see him?*

"Come. Eat. Woman," he shouted. She looked in his direction, but there was no movement. He would have to go to her. With a grunt, he glanced around.

No one was watching. He could be kind.

Ultan's guilt returned as he handed her the meager offerings. She took them, but neither ate nor drank. He found a stool, sat her down, and touched the bread to her lips. Blood caked on her delicate mouth. Despite her sodden dress, she did not shiver.

"Eat."

His words were from her language. He was sure he used the right ones. Old Finnegan, the skilled metalworker, was his teacher, and he was from her country. Ultan would learn more from Finnegan. Sonas ignored Ultan and watched his two younger cousins wrestling with everyone.

He sighed. Then yawned. Sonas did, too. On his hunkers, Ultan nudged Sonas to eat again. She nibbled the bread.

Progress.

He sniffed. *She stank. Bad. Of piss. Death. Perhaps shit?* His nose wrinkled, but he stayed by his prize. He heard her slurp the ale and wince at the taste. His father's grog was known to be strong.

"Fire," Ultan said and pointed at the pit. His mother's favorite dog sat next to her foot and licked the dirty skin. He saw her foot tremble as she reached down a morsel of bread to the dog.

Ultan didn't stop her, and the dog snatched the food.

"Dog," he muttered at Sonas.

Why would she not look at him? Why did he want her to forgive him? She should thank him for taking her from such a father.

"Good," Ultan said, smiling.

"No," Sonas whispered. "Bad."

He heard and understood. His innards curled.

Yes, he stopped Loki's temper as they came ashore, but he took a free woman away from all she knew. And for what?

He saw the drops on her hand. Tears. The dog licked them off. More came.

"Drink," he ordered.

She did.

Ultan watched the fire cracking and his people laughing, and then glanced at the falling sorrow from the stranger. The ropes blistered her hands, but they remained smooth. *She did not know a woman's hard work, but she could weave?* But he saw Sonas O'Neill had servants. She would not cook or clean. She was virginal, too. There were no children to care for.

What could she do in Upvhal? Freya was a jealous wife, but he did not blame her, because when Jarl Borg paid attention to her, he was furious.

If he took another woman Freya promised to leave him, and divide their wealth. Freya was a good fertile female and had given him three sons. She had cared for his daughter, too, before the fever took the infant.

"Why?" Sonas sobbed.

Ultan could not answer Sonas' cries. Even if he knew the words, he would not admit the desperate pull inside him. No matter what his heart said, Ultan was sure about what must happen. Odin wanted a sacrifice and Ultan needed a special gift for the All-Father. A powerful death could make Ultan the Fearless the greatest warrior for generations.

Chapter Three

The Brute

The Brute who carried Sonas ashore into this foul-smelling place was a leader. The women flocked to care for him, the men all sought his attention, and the couple seated at the top of the longhouse were fond of him. There was a resemblance between him and a few of the young wrestling boys, and they all encouraged The Brute's woeful singing. He was called Ultan, for they all chanted his name while battering on the sturdy wooden tables for more of the dreadful noise.

The dog had the right idea. He slunk into the shadows and stole food. Sonas lay with her back against the wall between the stacks of apples and what smelled like barrels of wheat. None of the people looked hungry and the favored animals chewing their cud or wandering through the tables all looked well cared for. Despite her exhaustion, Sonas was on high alert. She needed to establish what was happening and how she would survive.

She peered around again. There were none of her kinfolk in the longhouse. If they'd survived the voyage and the storms, they were not here to comfort her.

Was she to become a mere slave?

Sonas' father stole slaves, but he did not keep many, for he was not rich enough to feed them. If they ran away, he rarely bothered to chase them. Sonas did not have a clear idea of what a Norse slave should look like. And none of these people were unhappy or maltreated.

The women ignored her, but she observed them intently. There were a few clad in leather, and they carried long knives in their belts. Some looked cleaner and wore elegant dresses. But no one dressed like the lady on the top seat. There was a mark inked on her slender neck and her light-colored hair was tightly braided, adorned with pretty beads and shells. A fine cloak covered her long tunic, and an intricately decorated brooch fastened them together. Even from a distance, she could tell the woman wore her great wealth with pride. *Was she their queen?*

The man to her left was an older version of The Brute. There were streaks of gray hair in his dark mountain of hair, but he was still a large, powerfully built specimen. He laughed with his whole body. People revered him. *Was he the king? Then Ultan was a prince?*

Sonas recognized certain words from their language, and she could ask someone to help her, but it was pointless. Instead, she cradled the dog's head and closed her eyes for a short while. She awoke to the sound of her name again. Ultan was on his feet. He staggered and called at the top of his lungs. The tone sounded like he was concerned. *For her? Humph!*

Sonas stood from the shadows on weak, sore limbs and she swayed to match his movements. He ordered her to come to him once more. *She would not be called like a dog. She would not budge for The Brute.*

Even though she was bleeding and still soaking, Sonas stood firm. She could no longer see because of her falling tears. The blurred outline of The Brute handed her more bread and a horn cup. Then he forced her to sit on the stool again. *This place even smelled dangerous. His bulk was intimidating. She was alone, bleeding, and damaged, and things could become worse. The gods should have drowned her with the others, for there was no hope left.*

His body shifted uneasily, and she waited for a blow, but none came. Then she cried all the more. *Why did he take her here? Away from all she knew? Surely he could see she was not a warrior woman nor a laborer for their homes and fields.*

As if reading her mind, he took her hand and examined the palm. His touch was gentle and tickled, but Sonas did not move. *She refused to look at him. What was he doing? Because of her injuries, he took her hand and examined her skin. Did they eat human flesh, as the stories said?*

A shiver shot down her spine, and she trembled with the cold. He sniffed the surrounding air again. She smelled of everything foul from the ship and the floor of the longhouse. She was far from the lady she once was. As he rolled her dress sleeve higher on her arm, Sonas fixed her gaze on the adornments in the rafters. Their carpenters were skilled. The curls, swirls, and interlacing patterns were everywhere. Heads of magical beasts ate the end of long snakes. They were beautiful. When The Brute whispered into her ear, she came back to reality.

What did he say?

"You will stay here," he whispered in her language. His breath stank of ale as he leaned closer. "Helga is a good lady. You will be her handmaiden until we go to Uppsala. I will come back for you."

Sonas held her breath. *A handmaiden?*

Ultan belched. Sonas waited. His voice was deep and calm. When he bellowed in the great hall, he sounded brutal. By her ear, he was different.

"Freya would kill you," he said. "Yes. She would. And you are special."

Sonas wiped the worry from her cheeks and sniffed. "Special?" Her voice broke, and she asked again. "I'm special?"

Then Ultan's brown eyes met hers. They were kind. She stared at the Brute's caring eyes, then at his square jaw, down the hair on his neck, back up the slope of his nose, and across the scars on his cheek. For a savage, he was handsome.

"Yes," he said with a slight smile. "Eat. Drink. Be safe."

At the sincere sign of kindness, Sonas' tears fell again. She hated showing weakness, but there was nothing she could do to stop them. His hard hand touched her cheek, and she flinched. Then tenderly he held her face like she was a bruised apple. Tilting her chin upwards, he squeezed slightly, urging her to look at him.

He smiled. "Yes?" he questioned. "You'll stay here until I come back?"

"I've no choice," Sonas replied. "I'll wait."

Chapter Four

Living Again

Her gaze regularly flicked across the expanse of the longhouse. *She had been a captive for four days and she was as safe as she could be...but she constantly surveyed the place...for him. The Brute! How could she care where he was? He tore her from all she knew and placed her in a strange and vicious land. She shouldn't and wouldn't forgive him. By all their gods, she would curse him...yes, she would...try to...hate him.*

Helga, the queen, saw to her wounds. The other women were respectful of Sonas. This was a blessing. Sonas needed people to like her. She was used to a certain level of acceptance and reverence. Despite her father's treacherous reputation, she held a high status. To fall low enough to sleep on the floor took its toll. Yet the queen's favorite dog clung to Sonas. *Perhaps he was guarding the queen against Sonas? But he was an adorable animal and her only comfort as she cried through the nights.*

Helga gave Sonas two sets of dry dresses, leather foot coverings, and underclothes. One dress was thicker and for everyday wear. A plain rough linen one for a taller woman, and the other was lighter for special occasions, and clung to Sonas' curves. The fabric and the embroidery on the cuffs and neckline were masterful.

The other maidens cleaned and styled her hair in braids. Sonas shed a tear. Her reflection in the shiny metal was new. Sonas looked like her captors.

Would she ever see Ireland again? Was she really in a new home? Forever? Her father sat in their settlement, rubbing his hands. He had got rid of his pagan child. Christianity had a lot to answer for. She would make him pay.

Queen Helga could not talk with her, but Sonas found a few words, and their time together was pleasant. Sonas could at least thank the mother of Upvhal. From what Sonas saw, Helga was a powerful woman who ruled equally with her husband. She was in sole charge when he left the fortress to hunt in the nearby forests or to fish or raid from the cluttered harbor. When Helga walked outside, her maidens surrounded her, and she did not venture far. The largest maiden tethered Sonas to her and her fierce gaze warned Sonas to behave.

The air outside was biting cold, for the winter was coming and the enormous trees behind the fort were almost bare. Sonas shivered without a cloak, but their march between the houses and hovels kept her blood pumping. People sold, mended, traded, and chattered. New sights, smells, and sounds were around each corner or open space. Even with her red hair, Sonas fitted in. No one noticed she was different, for there were people of many-colored skins in Upvhal, and they all bowed their heads to the queen and her maidens.

Helga's duties started at sunrise. Therefore, on the second morning, Sonas was there amongst the first of the handmaidens. There were five, and they saw to Helga's every need. Some carried weapons and knew how to use them. They were trusting of a stranger, and Sonas craved more of the queen's approval and smiles. She was on trial and needed to pass whatever these tests were to survive. One slash from a blade and her life would end. And while Sonas lay and looked at the carpentry in the ceiling, she pondered how her life could be a lot worse. Yet she would still return home to kill her father. He sold her so his illegitimate children would rise. Or perhaps because she refused to marry. *Whatever the reason, she would gut him like a fish! She would not sleep on a sack in the corner forever.*

Days spread into turns of the moon, and Sonas found laughter again. Behind the double doors in the inner chamber, Sonas was safe. She also heard more of the important information in Upvhal. Helga was privy to everything. Messengers were constant, and in the afternoons she and her husband Arden held council with their best warriors and nobles. One evening out of every seven, Helga sat beside Arden and together they ruled on disputes within Upvhal. Sonas did not understand exactly what was happening, but if she listened and observed, she could guess. Sometimes, Ultan's name passed in conversation and Sonas held her breath. She strained to hear the information but mostly she learned nothing.

Why did the eldest son of a powerful Norseman have an Irish name? Ultan was a name from a province in the North called Ulster. There was a definite connection between him and her homeland, but there was also a thread of something binding him to her. Despite his absence, she recalled his touch still, sensed his eyes upon her, and his protection from afar. When was her Northman coming back?

But Sonas was busy, because she was excellent at

needlework and anything involving intricate artistry. She used thin charcoal embers to draw elaborate patterns onto linen for the blacksmith and carpenter. Most Vikings were involved in tasks for daily survival. Sonas was lucky to have the time to scribble and lose herself in the process of creating something. The designs she produced were Celtic and reflected what she saw in the Christian monks' books and metalwork, but some of her ideas came from Norse fireside stories, too.

When the weaving started in the longer evenings, Sonas showed how she was an expert weaver. The women came to Sonas to learn different techniques, and she assimilated their methods into her own. There was no time to be lonely or homesick. Despite the language barrier, Sonas had many new friends. Although it was not the same as being with her cousins or comrades back home, she found support in her new life.

She called the dog Gruff, and he remained her loyal companion, day and night. She washed him when she had her time in the handmaidens' bathing barrel.

When the snows came, people rarely left the blazing fire pit. The smaller houses outside the main dwelling were for animals, but a few found their way inside the warmer longhouse. Because the Upvhal people were kind, they did not put out these stowaways.

As a handmaiden, the warriors or menfolk did not touch Sonas. A low-born man was disrespectful if he even met a handmaiden's gaze. Sonas welcomed the status, for although she saw no ill-treatment, some slaves endured harassment when the men got drunk (and this was often).

In the evenings, she sat on her stool to the left of Helga's throne, and here Sonas had the best firelight for her embroidery. She could also hear and see most of the things people would gossip about the next day. She was more proficient in their tongue and spoke more confidently.

"I visited the blacksmith, Sonas," Helga said. "He says if I insist, he will show you how he melts our precious metals and makes our jewelry."

Sonas' heart thumped. She had wanted to learn metalwork for some time. People revered Old Celtic Finnegan and his fine craftsmanship. Some of Sonas' designs were in his workshop, and he asked for her to come to the forge.

Sonas leaned over and gripped Helga's hand in thanks, but a group of smelly warriors trooped forward to leave their spoils at the king's feet. The talk of battles always troubled Sonas, and she stitched her garment instead.

"You learned our ways quickly," Helga said and tapped Sonas' arm. "You surprised our Ultan."

Sonas murmured in agreement, paused her embroidery, and gasped. For there, covered in mud and snow…was the one she waited for…Ultan the Fearless.

Chapter Five

The Brute Returned

His mother said, "Yes. Here is Sonas."

Ultan shook his head. He could not remember when he saw the maiden before. He was never good with time, but many moons circled over since he'd held her hand and looked into her blue eyes. He dreamed of and imagined Sonas more than he should. And got hard with desire. *Was she the same woman? Elegant. Clean... Beautiful.*

"She's changed. There has never been a moment's bother with her. Sonas is an excellent handmaiden, and she is a caring, free-woman of Upvhal," Helga said with a huge smile.

This was high praise. Helga didn't like everyone, especially those who could threaten her power. And beauties like Sonas always attracted Arden's eye. Helga had been Arden's mistress for many years, while Ultan's mother stood by...until she went to be with the gods.

"And yes, she is still virtuous," Helga said with a raised voice. "As I have said, Sonas gave us no trouble at all. Her eyes and hands remained busy making beauty for herself, the settlement, and our cloth stores. She's talented."

Sonas' pale cheeks blushed, and she touched her mouth.

By the gods, she was a meek beauty! He chose well when he bought her. And she was modest as well as chaste.

"Stop staring," Loki said and stuck an elbow into Ultan's ribs. "She's a Celt. A bitch. Nothing more."

Sonas understood because she glared at Loki. Ultan chuckled. She then cursed Loki under her breath. She used their language already. *How clever...and damn feisty.*

Ultan's cock twitched. *By the gods, he still wanted the wench... to kiss her mouth...feel her under him...*

"Bring us something for the men," Arden ordered Sonas.

"She is not a slave," Ultan said. "We can wait for the servants."

Loki groaned and took off his outer cloaks and furs. The weather had been dangerous, and Loki moaned all the way. He preferred his warm home and hated the trek across the mountains. But Ultan had a purpose, and his men did not question him. *Thank the gods.*

When the singing and story-telling started, Ultan sat beside Sonas. She did not speak and stitched a long piece of cloth. *A new dress, perhaps?*

"Please tell me we have not come back for you to sink your cock into her?" Loki whispered. "You've not taken your eyes off the witch since we got here. Did you not have enough women in Fiordland?"

"I had forgotten all about her. But she's cleaned well, no?" Ultan whispered. "She's not tall or lean, but she's hefty and her shapely breasts are nice?"

Loki grunted and gulped from his drinking horn.

Ultan sang when asked, and he performed for Sonas. *Helga clapped, but Sonas did not bother. She did not smile either. Not once. There was no joy in her face. He made her sad, lonely, and yes, she was afraid.*

"Sonas is the same with every man who shows any interest in her," Helga whispered when Ultan sat beside her. "Your father flirted with her, too, but she ignored him. He became inflamed. They were the gossip for a long while."

Ultan grimaced. "You're a patient woman, Helga," he admitted. "Freya has tired of me and returned to her mother's birthplace. I don't blame her, but I gave her a portion of my hoard and she took two of our sons. The twins. The same could happen here. You would be within your rights to leave Arden."

"I'm happy," Helga said. She paused, fixed her shoulder brooch, she drank more ale, and spoke again. "I've good status here and want for nothing. Your father is a provider and is young enough to go hunting and raiding. Then I have full control. He has no brother left, and I will rule Upvhal when he goes to Valhalla. I can wait."

Ultan snorted. *Women schemed ahead. And yet, she did not see him as a rival? She spoke of power. Did she forget he was the eldest son? Perhaps she still trusted him. There was no strife between them…yet.*

"What will you do without Freya?" Helga asked.

"When I'm gone, Bjorn is in charge."

"That's not what I meant," Helga said with a wry smile. "Who will take Freya's place? Is there someone else? Or did you just wish to be away from Freya, Ultan the Fearless?"

"There's no one. We were never a love match. But she gave me sons. She can go. I hope the twins return, though. I miss them."

"Why come over the mountains in the snow?" Helga asked. "We're glad to see you, and delighted with the gifts you brought, but you traveled at a strange time of year. People will wonder."

"I wanted to trade and prepare for Uppsala. With Freya leaving, my hoard is lacking."

"Ah!" Helga said, raising an eyebrow. "And you want some of your prizes from the raids?"

Ultan's jaw clenched, and he took a long drink from the horn cup. "If you agree, I would take some, yes."

"The prizes are yours to take," Helga said, and beckoned for more food.

"No more. I might burst," Ultan said.

"You look well, Ultan," Helga said with a wink. She rubbed his belly. They were close in age, but she was not flirting. "There must be some woman for you?" she teased, looking around. "You'll be cold tonight in your old bed. Take one of my handmaidens. My gift to you."

Ultan gasped. Helga never treated her maidens like whores. She winked again.

"No," Ultan said. "You've been drinking. You don't mean it."

"I do." Helga laughed. "Like your father, you've probably bedded most of them anyhow."

Ultan attempted to take the cup from Helga, but someone got there first.

"No more," Sonas whispered. "To bed, my Queen."

Ultan rose, but Sonas shoved him back. "No," she said. "Sit, enjoy the night."

Was he like a dog?

But then she smiled. *He needed her to give him another reassuring, sweet one.* Then, to inflame him more, as she left, her warm arse brushed his crotch, *and he longed...He should thrust...Was that lavender oil he could smell in her hair?*

Helga and Sonas linked arms and left the great hall. Ultan watched them leave. He closed his drooling mouth.

****

When Sonas returned, they might be alone. Where did she sleep? He could insist Helga fulfilled her promise. He should. She offered one of her handmaidens. Why was he quick to refuse?

No matter how hard he wished and waited...No matter how patient his cock was...Sonas did not return. Dawn shone into the longhouse when Ultan tiptoed into the inner chamber and passed his father's bed.

What he saw in the furs stopped his breath...

Chapter Six

His Woman

Daylight rarely reached the inner chamber of the longhouse, but the other handmaidens left one of the double doors open. They needed more light to get Helga dressed. She was not cooperative.

"Arden?" Helga shouted. "Where is he? I refuse to meet the farmers with their winter tributes alone. He is not a jarl yet, and he still acts like one."

Helga was not a queen in the Norse world. But her title didn't matter. To Sonas, she was one and her husband's behavior was disrespectful. He left the important meetings to Helga, and she was suffering pitifully under the strain. That was why the previous night, Sonas snuggled into Helga's nice straw mattress to embrace her mistress.

"I was only teasing Ultan," Helga admitted before she nodded off. "He wants you to be a virgin. He'll not take you against your will. I wouldn't let him. You're safe."

"Hush. Sleep," Sonas said as she rubbed Helga's hair and shoulders. Helga snored in a drunken slumber while Sonas thought about what Ultan wanted from her. She was still pondering as she rose before everyone else and did her early chores.

A virgin? Was she to be his mistress? He had a

wife… Why had he brought her to Upvhal? Whatever his wants were, he was back.

She asked others how long he would be. They told her, "When the ice and snow thaw, all will change." *But this was many moons away. Yet here he was. Why? The Brute constantly stared, too. Concentrating and ignoring him was difficult. Why did he affect her so much? She barely knew him, and he owned her. She was one prize from his raids. Slaves were good currency. Did he intend to sell her on to another man as a breeding woman? Would he take her back to his home, to his wife?*

Her stomach ached with worry. Sonas saw other men take a second wife or a *kærasta* to his bed, but it rarely ended well. The women rarely agreed, and things got messy. Helga judged many disputes, and they were because of *ást*, or lack thereof.

Could she lie with Ultan? Perhaps. He interested her. A lot. She was not afraid of penetration, if the partner was one she could choose for herself.

Cheekily, Sonas peeked at Ultan as he slept farther along in the wooden bed with the drapes. The thick material was to ward off draughts and prying eyes, but he did not drop them from their ties. His bare chest and naked thighs were some sight as Sonas edged closer. His long, black hair was loose and wild-looking, and his mouth was slightly open with a muscular arm extended over his head. *Without clothing, he looked appealing…*

If only his other hand and fur did not shield his modesty.

Sonas ogled Ultan for a long while. The others busied themselves in the great hall, and there was time for her to gawp. *If she waited a while longer, she might see all of him…he would be nice…*

Sonas got lost in her imaginings and thoughts. After a few heartbeats she realized Ultan's eyes were open.

Shit!

"Good morning," he said and yawned, moved the fur, and gave her a spectacular view of what she was waiting for. He was erect.

Oh no! Despite being caught, she couldn't stop looking.

"You're bright red," Ultan added with a laugh. "Why?"

Norsemen were not easily embarrassed, but she was mortified. Like a thief, she turned to run, but he leaped naked from the bed and was in front of her before she escaped.

If she hadn't seen the cock, she wouldn't want to look. Or want him. No, she would not peek.

"You've seen me now," he whispered. "Open your eyes."

She would not!

Then he cupped her elbow and brought her frame closer to his naked body. She tingled at his touch. He smelled lovely. Like warm straw and leather. His breath tickled her cheek as he leaned and whispered, "You waited for me?"

She nodded. *There was no choice, and she was foolish. Why did she melt like snow when he was around? He owned her. Stole her. Bought her. Whatever he did...he took her from all she knew, and yet when he was near, she was weak. And stupid. What was he doing?*

She smelled his manly aroma and opened one eye to see his mouth close to her nose. His beard grazed across her cheek as he wrapped his brawny arms around her. She felt his hard cock on her belly, and her chin rested on his solid chest.

Oh my!

"I thought about you," he said. "Worried, too."

He was concerned. Well, good. He should have been. He was hot and when he was close…She was on fire.

"Helga likes you," he said.

"She's a good woman." Sonas raised her arms to drape them awkwardly around his waist. She could make her fingers meet, but he was broad. There was such a fiery energy between them. Yet he shivered when she touched his back.

Was he giddy and breathless, too? What did he want? She desired…

"I better get dressed," he said, but neither of them moved. "I'm glad we're here together. You're safe with me."

She was secure. Since he sat her on the stool the first night, she trusted he would not harm her.

"Yes," she said and laid her cheek fully on his heart. She heard the beat.

Had the thump gotten faster, like her own? She liked being in his strong protective arms. His body wanted her.

"Do you always sleep with Helga?" he asked.

"No," she said, smiling because he sounded jealous.

"Good."

"I sleep on the floor with Gruff."

"Who?"

"The dog."

He chuckled light-heartedly, and she did, too.

"Did you hear Helga's gift to me last night?"

Oh yes. She heard, but she would not admit

anything.

"Helga was silly. Because you are mine to have any time I want," he said.

Sonas moved out of the embrace and shrugged off her owner as if he were an old cloak. "I'm a free woman of Upvhal. Helga said." She forced his bulk even farther away.

"That was only until I came back," Ultan said.

Sonas ran.

But The Brute called after her, shouting something that sounded very much like "...and you are my woman!"

Chapter Seven

Deep Decisions

Ultan curled his fingers into a fist. He broke the spell between them and ruined his chances. After many attempts, he yanked on his britches. His feet stuck in his boots. He fell over twice. By the time he was shirtless in the great hall, Sonas was long gone. He cursed loudly.

The servants fussed around him, brought him oats and heated the goat's milk he liked for his morning meal. He stretched to ease a pain from between his shoulder blades. Sonas did things to him. Stirred his cock for one thing and turned his mind foggy. He cursed again.

By Odin, he would not care for a slave! For this was what she was. With all her airs, her father traded her. No matter how beautiful or high-born she was, she was his property. His píka*! If he wanted to romp on her belly he would do it.*

Helga arrived with an amused smile. As she sat, he recognized the smell of the foul-smelling headache remedy she carried in her cup and wrinkled his nose.

"Will you help me with the tributes today? There is no sign of your father. I'm tired and may need you." Helga moaned.

"Too much mead last night?" Ultan asked.

"Yes."

He slopped a small wooden spoon about in his hot

oats.

"I saw Sonas leaving," Helga said.

"Humph."

"I know you treat her like she is just another wench," Helga whispered. "But you know she is special."

"I don't want to talk about Sonas."

"You need to decide what you're going to do. Sonas has no real understanding of our beliefs and does not know what happens at Uppsala. If she is going there with you, we will all need to prepare her. And if she is going before the priests, then…"

"I don't know…," he blurted out.

"Either way. You need to decide. I have grown fond of Sonas and I'm not sure I'll allow…"

"She's mine!" Ultan said and slammed down his spoon. He felt childlike, demanding a toy back.

Helga smirked.

He balled his fist.

She was certain she was winning. He was losing his temper…again. Women tortured him.

"Sonas is well-bred. She is excellent at all she does. Despite all the work I give her, she betters herself, learning sword skills, metalwork, and remedies. She made a potion for me, with the healer, long before I got up. I know you want some powerful gift for Odin, but I see Sonas as a *munud* or love for you. A wife. There, I've said my piece. Think about this." She stood.

Ultan sighed. "I've considered already." He looked up at the woman he called Mother and then peered around. "I've thought of nothing else. She is on my mind all the time. Like a sickness. I'm under her spell." They were alone, and he continued. "I came back for Sonas. Nothing else is in my soul. I only think of her."

"I know," Helga said with the same satisfied look. "She is one of your birth mother's people. You will have a strong connection. Her kin's blood flows in your veins too. Even Arden knows you have feelings or *ást* for her. I think this is one reason he did not take her against her will. Which we both know was possible when you left her here. He does not care about the consequences of raping a virgin."

He never thought of the danger Sonas was in. Helga could have only done so much. He should have realized. And this morning...he scared her. Of course, she did not understand he cared because he did not tell her.

"We're strangers," he said. "I forget this. If only I had told her I would protect her. I mean her no harm. But she does not see..."

Helga flopped into the chair, tiredness obvious in her eyes. "What age are you? Have you any sense at all? Did you or did you not buy the poor woman as an unwitting sacrifice? You are harming her. Aren't you still sitting here thinking of taking her for your ambitions?"

Ultan could not speak. His mind and heart whirled.

"You wanted a glorious offering. I understand. But then, you left her here. You abandoned her, left her injured, cold, and confused. Never bothered to tell any of us of your decision. And as Sonas is a good and clever woman, she learned our language, made friends, and became secure and happy again..."

"I couldn't take her to Freya. She'd have gutted her like a fish. What else could I do?"

"You could have left her in her homeland," Helga hissed and eyed him with disdain. "You could have slit her throat, thrown her into the sea with her kin, or sacrificed her the minute you came to Upvhal. But no! Instead, you play God with her future and her emotions. She is not a goat, dog, or animal. To me, she is a free woman with valuable skills. Make your choice, Ultan the Fearless. But I am warning you, I may not agree with your decision."

Helga slapped his shoulder and then the back of his head. "That was a knock because you are a stupid arse and the eldest son of your even more clueless father. You will help me with the morning tributes. You shall be of use and learn about life."

Ultan dressed in his best attire and sat in his father's seat. He surveyed the great hall. There were many families from their lands coming in with produce for their leader. They pledged their loyalty to his family for the promise of protection and future glory. As Helga worked, he watched. She was a responsible woman. She held the whole of Upvhal in her palm. They acted upon every word. Every smile was like gold to those before her. His other brothers, and half brothers, were a long way from ambitions. A few more raids and favor from the powerful jarls and his dreams of glory would happen. He needed to stay patient and fearless.

What was Sonas' value? As a sacrifice, Odin would be pleased and bless him. There was no question. However, if he had a wife like Helga, he could achieve as much, or maybe even more, than his father. His first wife, Freya, was lazy and did not care about his ambitions. But a woman with traits like Helga could keep his interests in Fiordland while he became a legendary jarl. Could Sonas be his kærasta? *She was still young and startled easily. She would toughen up. Sonas would become a Norsewoman. But if she was good and clever, he would teach her their ways. By the gods, he would.*

Ultan dragged his mind back to his duties. He presented warrior bracelets to the young boys coming of age and blessed twelve new babies. When one farmer offered his fearful daughter as a handmaiden, something snapped inside Ultan. "Not unless she agrees," he shouted.

The man appeared insulted, and the daughter recoiled with shock.

"Decide," Ultan demanded.

The girl asked, "What will I do?"

"Decide."

As he waited for a reply, Ultan made some deep decisions of his own.

Chapter Eight

A Norse's Proposal

Sonas did not want to return to the longhouse, but she hadn't eaten all day. *The Brute would be there. No doubt, the lovely farming folk she met during the day brought many fine garments and furs to the Brute's feet.*

"Time for you to go," Old Finnegan said as he put handfuls of sawdust on the smelting fire. "Helga said you could stay, but the tributes will be over, and she will need you. Are you listening, girl?"

Sonas nodded and wore the shawl Finnegan gifted her earlier. The garment belonged to his late wife, and still smelled of the Norse woman who took him out of slavery. She sold Finnegan's skills to her people. After just a few years, though, she walked into the sea during a terrible storm. Finnegan became "old" overnight, with his hair graying all at once. People said he was always grumpy, but since she had left him alone, he had a woeful temper.

"Get home with you then," he said in the old words she grew up with, "and take the hound with you. Nobody else has an animal stuck to their heels. I've fallen over him and that's dangerous here."

Despite his protests, Old Finnegan ruffled Gruff's hairy head.

Sonas smiled."Thank you for today. I love hearing

our language." She opened his door latch. The evening was dark, and icicles hung from the pitched wooden roof. Outside smelled damp, and she shivered. "I don't want to go…might be the warmth in here, but maybe I love your wonderful company."

He chuckled. "Stop with your teasing and get off to where you belong."

She complained to him earlier about her kidnap and not feeling totally at ease in her new home. "I know," he said. "But there are worse fates, and Upvhal is a nice place. Especially in better weather. And you're in the Great Hall. The Thorvald clan is making something of themselves. Accept your fate."

"I never hear their Thorvald name. Only 'The Fearless.' "

"They are clever," Finnegan said. "If you say something often enough, you come to believe the words."

Sonas asked about his own Celtic home, but he shook his head. "I don't recall," he said. "Wait, watch how the molten gold flows into the mold."

When the time came for Sonas to leave, she paused in the doorway. "I'm going then," she called and peered into the snowy darkness. "I may be back soon to see how the swords are finished and how you polish those brooches."

"Good night and may all the gods protect you," Finnegan shouted as she shielded her head against the slanting sleet. She enjoyed her time in the forge. Emotion gripped her belly.

Was she afraid? Or nervous or something else?

The guards opened the door, and then they moved into the bitter night. She vowed to take them some warmed milk and rum later. After the activity of the day in Upvhal, the longhouse was relatively quiet. She tossed off the shawl and large flecks of snow drifted onto the floor rushes. Gruff shook his ears, making a pleasant flapping noise.

She was freezing even though she wore her two gifted dresses together these days. Although her homeland was in the damp west of Eire, there was nothing as bitter as Danish snow.

There were a few warriors and servants at the tables nearest the blazing fire pit. Some others were asleep in the reeds and straw beds along the walls. The doors to the inner chamber were closed. Candles flickered in various places, but the center of the longhouse was the most visible. A quick survey of the space told Sonas the man she sought was missing. A maidservant stirred the cauldron on the main fire and beckoned Sonas. The aroma of salted fish stew greeted her.

"Yum," she said as her mouth watered. "Thank you." She tore off a huge chunk of bread from the loaf on the table and sipped from the nearest horn cup.

"Thirsty work today, Sonas?" one warrior asked.

"I was in the forge. Hot, heavy work. Is this yours?" she replied and showed him what she believed to be honeyed milk.

"No. Not mine," he said. "I think it's Ultan's."

"Of course, I'd choose his," Sonas muttered but drank on. *Lovers drank from the same cup.* There was no sign of The Brute. The cup's contents, and the plate of dried fruits, were hers. "Where is my lord and master then?" she asked.

"If you mean me, I'm here," Ultan's booming voice said from the group.

How had she missed him? His back was to her. She should sense where he was…

"Oh." She blushed crimson. Her hand touched her warm neck. "I did not see you there."

"Huh," he grunted.

The men elbowed each other. Gruff growled and rubbed against her thigh. The others enjoyed her discomfort. This was awful. At least Gruff was on her side.

Her hungry stomach reminded her she needed to eat. She took her bowl of stew as far away from the men as the cold would allow and sat and stared into the fire.

What would happen? Would The Brute let her eat in peace?

The maidservant gave Gruff a large goat's hip bone, and he gnawed. Sonas devoured the contents of her bowl, too. She guzzled a few heaped spoonfuls to finish the stew and used the bread to wipe the vessel clean. As she set all on the table, someone placed a full cup beside her. "Here," Ultan said and pushed honeyed milk closer, but he still held the cup. "An offering," he said with a big smile.

What was she going to do? What should she say? His strong scent was probably from the heat of the fire and the nightly wrestling contests. She missed his bare chest, and she liked to watch the rippled muscles wriggle and gleam.

"They tell me you've given me a new name," he whispered. "Ultan the Brute. Ha."

Her fingers trembled and brushed off his as she accepted his offering. Energy flowed between them and hurt like a spark from the fire. He yanked his hand back, too, as if injured.

She nestled hers against her breasts. "I must go and undress Helga and see to her needs," she said, for something to fill the awkwardness.

"She's in bed already. A long time ago."

"Was she looking for me? Is she angry?"

"No. Don't worry. You were at the forge, and she has a new handmaiden."

"What?"

"I'm back," he said, "and a family offered their girl today."

He placed her braided hair over her shoulder and sat to gaze directly into her eyes.

"This is good news for you, Sonas. I'm here to protect you and when you agree..." he whispered, coming even closer, "...and when you allow, I want you to be my *kærasta*, my woman."

Chapter Nine

A Throbbing Scar

Ultan looked around for something to wallop. He just asked her to be his. In reply, she got up and took hot honeyed mead out to the men on guard. The scar on his temple hurt when he was angry. He rubbed it. *Ouch! Did she not know how good an offer it was?*

As ever, she walked with elegance. *She was sure of herself. Tall. Strong. In charge. She was a good choice. His instincts in choosing her were right. In awe, he stared at her, making more of her potions. As a Norse woman, she would be smaller and more rounded than the others. But was this a good plan? He'd promised her to Odin. Everyone always knew Ultan's destiny because a seer had foretold that Odin would grant him glorious victories in battle and make him a conquering jarl. How would it come true if he stayed in Upvhal, under Helga's rule, in the bed of a slave? Maybe his cock was leading him astray?*

She tucked a hair behind her tiny ears. He waited for her to smile at him. Finally, she did, and the smile was worth a hoard of gold. *Her worry was melting with his concerns. Good.* The others left to sleep. They became bored while waiting for the two of them to mate.

He was alone by the fire and all he wanted was for Sonas to tell him her thoughts. As if his will alone made it happen, she returned carrying two steamy goblets.

"To help keep us warm," she said and gazed at the floor.

"You've learned our words well," he told her with pride.

"I had some words before..." She stopped.

"Before we took you."

"Yes."

Could he grab her into his arms and devour her? Why wait? They were alone. "I don't know why or how you survived, but you did. Your fate was to thrive in Upvhal," he said.

"I believe so." Her tongue licked the froth from her lips and drove him wild with desire.

He stood to walk away. He needed to busy himself with something. His hands wanted to be on Sonas. "Talk to me," he said, even though it was the last thing he enjoyed when alone with a woman.

"About what?" she said.

"Anything," he muttered through gritted teeth and petted the mutt of a dog who never left her side. "I like stories, but I find conversations difficult. With you, I'm lost. I want to know what you're thinking. Then, I don't. You make me nervous. Talk."

"My people are the best storytellers in the world. Better than Vikings," she said, but her eyes would not meet his. "I miss home."

"Why? I provide well. You must have everything you want here?"

"With respect, no, I don't," she whispered.

"What do you miss?"

"Not what. Who," she said.

His breath stopped. *She had a man of her own. She*

was of age and her father wanted rid of her. He must not have approved of the match. She loved another.

"I miss my people. I had friends and family. Everyone is kind to me here. I have status and am well fed and safe. But I'm lonesome."

He nodded and ventured the question, "A love match? Do you miss him?"

"Oh, no!" she gasped. "There's no one."

The relief. How pretty her eyes were when they shone in the firelight?

"You're happy?" she asked.

He wiped a hand across his beard. The emotion must have shown on his face. "Yes," he admitted. "I get jealous."

She smiled as she clutched the shawl around her shoulders.

"You need new clothes. Why hasn't someone given you new clothes? Did I not see you sewing something?" he said, picking at the holes in her threadbare dress. *She wore something bulky underneath. This was why he couldn't tell what her figure was like anymore.*

"I mend Helga's garments. To have some new ones of my own, I must have something to trade," she said with a sniff.

"No wonder you're shivering. Come here."

He embraced her. The dog growled, but Ultan still covered Sonas with his bulky arms and snuggled his nose into her hairline. "Now we will get warm."

She sighed as he sniffed her hair, and they cuddled closer. The red strands floating free smelled good and were soft against his lips and cheek. *He liked how her fingers lay on his belt. If only she would undo his clothes. She was small, but fitted him perfectly. They would be good together. Exceedingly good.*

Without thinking, he scooped her up just as he had carried her from the ship all those months ago. She did not protest, but the dog's mouth gripped his leg. Ultan cursed until she whispered, ordering his release. Ultan's soul soared to the gods in thanks.

S*he wanted him, too. There was* munud *or desire between them. They could be as one person for hours this night. He would plunder her over and over until dawn.*

His groin was on fire, but he carried her quietly into the inner chamber. His childhood bed looked great. He set her down and flicked the ties open. The curtains fell around the bed. They were alone again. Quiet. Panting in anticipation. Just them. He would...

"Can I ask something?" Sonas said.

Ultan removed his outer fur, his short tunic, and his undershirt. He scratched his chest hair. She would like his muscles. Women always did. "Ask away," he said and propped on the long feather-filled sacks.

"You are powerful," she said as she wrung those tiny hands in her lap.

"Not as much as I would like. But if I had a good woman, this would change."

She glared. Her green eyes reminded him she was troublesome. "If I had a good match. We might make power together," he said. *If only she would come closer. The night was freezing. He wanted her naked and burning under him.*

"Do you mean it?" she asked, breaking his daydreams. "Are you just telling me these things to lie with me?"

"What?" he gasped. "A Norse's word is his promise. His oath. Do you not understand?" He sidled beside her on the straw mattress. "Sonas. On my honor as a warrior, I want you to be my *kærasta*. You and I will make sons, and you will lead me to greatness. This is what the gods and I want."

"Why me?" she asked and held him at arm's length.

"I don't know."

She smirked. *She thought him less clever than her. He did not have fancy words. She was right.*

The scar in his temple throbbed almost as much as his cock.

As if to help him, she, too, lay against the pillows and sighed. She paused and then said, "Before I agree, I think you should know...I'm not who you think I am..."

Chapter Ten

A Norse's Bed

Next to Ultan's naked chest, Sonas lay and found herself distracted. Since arriving in Upvhal, Ultan's hairy muscles were Sonas' favorite sight. The beauty of the ships in the bay, the dewy grass, and the smoky, quiet settlement in the morning, were all lovely, but his chest was the best view of all.

How was a woman to concentrate and make her fate a good one with such a body and lustful looks burning a passion inside her? A once loathsome savage was sincere as she peered at his handsome face in the dark. *Did he want her as an equal? Impossible.* Yet here she sat on a Norse's bed with all the world stretching out before her.

Gruff joined them, but Ultan insisted he lay at the bottom and away from him.

"Fleas," he protested and scratched at the hair around his gorgeous nipples.

"He does not have any," Sonas promised. "I check."

"Explain to me who you are then," he asked. "And don't fret. I'm not easily shocked."

He took her hand and ran his calloused fingers through hers. She clenched her thighs in pleasure. If holding his hand thrilled her, she would drown in his kisses. She gulped. The anticipation and worry of what he might think sent her heartbeat racing.

"Tell me all," he said and kissed the back of her hand.

The gesture was tender, and Sonas closed her eyes. When she looked, he grinned, nodding for her to speak.

"My father is a Christian. A follower of Jesus Christ," Sonas started, praying inwardly to the god of the night for protection from yet another man in her life.

"I've heard of them," Ultan replied with a yawn. "Are you one of these Christians?"

"Never."

"Good. Hurry up with your talking."

He leaned closer, and unnerved her more. She would give in to those lips, eventually.

"My father did not like me," she said. "Never did. But I displeased him and his religion, and I made him angry."

"What did you do?"

"I don't have the right words to explain. The Norse words I mean…"

"Try."

"I've had lovers. With men and women. Like all at once," she blurted out.

Ultan sat bolt upright. He still held her hand, only the grip was tighter.

"I know Vikings do it, too, sometimes," she went on. "I've heard these things."

He nodded, but his eyes were wide. She could see the whites of them and his mouth curled at the sides.

"I've many secrets," she whispered.

Ultan coughed nervously. "I see," he said. "You're not a virgin or *píka*, then?"

"No."

"Well, this is wonderful news," he said with a wide

45

grin. "And is probably why your father wanted you gone?"

"Umm, yes. One reason."

"And is there more you want to tell me?" Ultan yawned again. "I'm tired."

Her potion would make him sleepy. She pursed her lips together. "Can I just ask you a few more questions? Please?"

Ultan shrugged in resignation.

"Will I have to leave Upvhal?"

"I live in Fiordland."

"And your woman?"

"She's gone. We are in disagreement."

"What?" Sonas asked in great relief.

"I know. I'm free and satisfied to be."

This was getting better and better. "What's the place like?"

"Not as big as Upvhal. However, in my own right, I've done well as a raider and trader. The king will soon give me my jarldom for saving his life. We will go to battle again soon. Then, with Odin's help, I'll prove myself again. He cannot ignore me forever."

Impressive. He'd made his own way despite his terrible father. They were alike in ways. He was ambitious, too. He was right they would make a good team. Wouldn't they? Could she overlook his savagery? She was used to viciousness in Eire. Her people raided each other for livestock and slaves. The Norse were just less bothered by the bloodshed. And he stole her. She was part of a bargain. He wanted her from the moment he saw her and said she was special. He was considerate and kept her safe.

"Take off your clothes and lie next to me," he

whispered.

"I want to." She untied her foot coverings, but her fingers were numbing with the cold.

"Let me help," he offered. But before he did, he kissed her cheek. Then, slowly, soft sensuous lips and a tickly beard with a warm breath came toward her mouth. "Let me kiss you," came the command. "Now."

The heat of his breath joined hers before their lips did. When his passion finally reached hers, the spark was like lightning. *A surge of desire locked them as one. Sonas got lost in his mouth and arms. She wanted him. Needed and deserved this handsome man to show his lust for her. She could not stop even if she wanted to, and why would she? All was glorious. His skin, his hardened desire. It was...wonderful.*

She panted as he pulled at her dresses and cursed. She forced her head out of the strained material and exposed her breasts to the cold. Her nipples ached while he slowly sucked one and then the other. Then he bit and gave her a sudden shot of pain and pleasure.

"Yes!" she moaned. He was excruciatingly good. She would fully surrender herself to the night and his fingers. There was nothing else she could do. She would lie there and let him do whatever he wished because she adored his mouth and what he was doing.

"More..."

"Look at you," he said as he swept coarse hands over her nakedness. She opened her legs for him. "And here," he whispered and slid into her wetness. "All for me?"

"Yes." She grinned. "Kiss me."

He smelled his fingers, licked them, and groaned, "You're my woman."

"Am I good?" she asked, to know her mind as much

as his. "You want me?"

In answer, he heaved his britches over his massive bulge. In the dark, Sonas reached for him, but he kissed her again.

"Wait." He kissed down her chest and belly. "Let me make you ready. Let me take you slowly. We have all night. And you will always yearn for me? Yes?"

Sonas lay back and groaned, "Yes. By my god, Dagda. Yes."

Chapter Eleven.

Watched

He lay on top of Sonas and slid between her spread thighs.

"Take me," she whispered and arched upward in need. *She was slick and ready for his cock. He made sure.* As he entered her, she came straining against his fingers and moaned loudly. He held over her mouth with his free hand. The others would wake. But Sonas was far gone, and her breathing sent her moans to a louder pitch. Inside was hot as she clenched around his fingers. *She knew what she wanted and held him there. Savoring all. Unbelievable. She was a goddess. Where was the meek slave he stole? His beauty was much better than any* píka. *She was hot. Bold. Like a clean whore. All his luck was naked under him. He would romp on her belly. When she admitted her past, he became fired up. She was a Norse. She had experience. And this showed. He would not use her as a sacrifice after all. She would be his* kærasta. *In his bed. Naked. Forever more.*

"Was that nice?" He stroked again between two warm and trembling thighs. She bit her lip and nodded. Those dreamy eyes were still half closed. *She adored this. He could not get enough! All he wanted was for her to need him like this over and over…And he'd not even taken her properly yet. He would be completely lost then.*

He gently circled her opening, and she panted, "Yes." He leaned up and positioned his tip there and thrust in slightly. *In order for him to be satisfied, he needed her to enjoy taking him, despite his size. If he entered her slowly, and with care, he would not lose his mind and heart...*

But when she sucked his tongue into her mouth, and he ravished her with his full-length, he couldn't resist. With a few deep thrusts, he spurted out his seed. "Argh!" he moaned. *By Odin, he emptied his sacks...this was the best plow of his life.*

He lay level with her breast, watching a bead of sweat heave with her breath. She ran her hands through his hair. Neither of them spoke. He wanted to stay there as they slept. He felt exhausted. His eyes closed. Sonas sighed. He lay on the pillows next to her dreamy eyes. She held his cheek.

"What are you thinking?" he whispered, resting his hand on her breast. Her skin tightened when he rubbed her nipple. "Talk."

She shrugged.

"This was...dangerous," he admitted. "I'm fearless most of the time. But this scares me. You scare me."

Her smile melted his heart.

"Sleep," she said and swiped her fingers over his eyes.

"This is real?" he asked.

"When you wake, we'll do it again."

"Promise?"

"Yes."

"Your word is your bond, my *kærasta*." He settled down to sleep. Content.

After many hours, he woke to her scent. Her hair, soft skin, and mouth soaked into his senses with their power. She curled into the furs. Lying nearer, he hoped she'd waken. But no, she slumbered. Her beautiful mouth was open slightly, her hair falling over slender shoulders, and her pink nipple peeking out of the covers at him. He ran a hand over her shapely leg and tucked the fabulous limb back under the furs. She stirred and smiled.

His kiss was to be a greeting. Nothing more. But she draped one arm over his shoulder, and he couldn't help himself. His tongue dipped into her mouth and his eager fists sank into the blankets. He found her nakedness and trailed down until he found her mound of hair.

"More?" he asked. "Again?" He rolled onto his elbows, and she let him between her legs. "I need back inside happiness." He entered her slowly. Each thrust was careful. He eased in and out until her juices came again. She bit his neck as he ground into her over and over. *He took time to sense all the special places inside his love. Yes. He loved her. Loved this. Loved. Loved. Loved.* "Sonas," he moaned.

Her nails gripped his back, and she tilted upward to greet his downward movements. *They fit together. He was meant to be there. Inside. All the way. In his woman. This would never end. This. Was. Valhalla on earth. His* kærasta.

She panted until she held her breath and fully tensed. Then she gave one long moan, louder than before. He took in her passion and erupted. Like a hot spring, he came, roaring into the pillow.

****

The sounds of servants woke Ultan. He reached for

Sonas and thanked the gods when he found her rump under the covers. "Come here," he said.

She turned to face him and lay flat on her stomach. He watched her yawn and allowed her to take his hand towards her bottom.

"Morning," she said with a yawn, and touched his face, felt across his soft lips, and tapped the tip of his nose.

He ran his rough hand along the curve of her arse and reached his happy place. He nuzzled her neck and rubbed fingers through the folds. "I could take you from behind?" he suggested. "Move up with my hard morning cock and take you again? Slide in here?"

Without realizing he was doing that very thing. The curve of her arse was warm and soft on his crotch. His thick length slid inside her and his hands grabbed shoulders and hair, pulling, heaving, gripping him deeper. He stuck her face into the pillow and his balls bounced off her tight, wet hole.

Someone shifted the curtain around his bed. *He couldn't stop and they...watched. Sonas was tight, and the sensation was too great, but he couldn't turn to tell them to leave. He could not stop! And whoever was peering at him could watch him fuck his woman. Cold air wafted over his clenching arse. They were still there.*

"Oh yes," he murmured into her ear.

Did Sonas know? Did she care?

"Argh!" he groaned. "Leave," he ordered, hoping they wouldn't until he finished. "Get up on your knees, Sonas," he said and gripped under her belly. She obeyed, and he fondled her bouncing breasts and thrust again and again. *If the person was still there, they would see their naked beauty and know what they could do together.*

With a long shout, he bucked his balls dry.

When he gathered himself and could look around, there was nobody there. Still on her knees, Sonas rubbed between her legs. She tilted back her neck, wet her fingers, and stuck them inside herself…and muttered his name as she came again. He never bedded a woman like her before, and they were only beginning…

Chapter Twelve

A Bath

Even with the sleeping potion, her Norse lover kept her awake all night with his lovemaking. The knowing glances from everyone in the longhouse were amusing. *But they couldn't know how many times they'd enjoyed each other. Even Sonas couldn't quite believe. And she wanted each one of those glorious sessions.*

Ultan got ready to hunt. He refused to kiss or touch her goodbye, saying, "If I do, I'll never leave."

The other handmaidens teased her a little, but then Helga appeared and all was quiet. Despite the time of year, Helga ordered the floor rushes to be replaced. The job was dirty and heavy. Men from the outhouses did the heavy sweeping and lifting, but the dusty work became sticky and horrid.

"Will we get time in the bathing barrels?" Sonas asked when the evening meal time came. Servants roasted chickens on spits over the main fire and her mouth watered. When they sat to eat, her hands, fingernails, and all exposed skin were filthy. She had ruined her only good dress.

Two of the men arranged enormous cauldrons and filled them with water. Then they added lavender and salt to each of the three bathing barrels and the women got ready to wash. Sonas had no change of clothes. She sat on a stool waiting on her Norse man to come home from the hunt, concerned at the state of her appearance.

All the happiness from last night was gone. She hadn't even clothes for her back. After all her hard work and lovemaking, she was exhausted and emotional.

"Have these," Helga said, giving Sonas a bundle of material. "You have worked hard for them." They were Helga's own. Sonas recognized the dress as one she mended and coveted. The thick fabric was a deep red, with flowing folds from the waist. There were many pockets, a fitted bodice with long sleeves, and a heavy matching cloak.

"Thank you," Sonas said. "I am grateful for your kindness."

"Let me help you," Helga said as she undressed Sonas for a change. The others finished drying themselves and left, chattering about who would style each other's hair.

Helga let Sonas' underskirt fall and stood back to look at her nakedness. Sonas felt exposed and covered her breasts.

"You are a beauty." Helga was breathless and flushed.

"Thank you," Sonas replied, unsure of how she would get into the barrel without help or the stool behind her mistress.

"Ultan has spoken with you?" Helga asked, her eyes still on Sonas' body. She walked around. "He told you about his decision?"

"I've given him mine."

"Your decision?" Helga asked with a smirk.

"Yes."

Helga threw back her head in laughter. Sonas

shivered from the new tension. There was an uncomfortable (yet interesting) pull between them.

"I'm shivering from the cold," Sonas lied. "Can I get in?" She pointed to the barrel.

Before Helga could answer, someone banged on the doors.

"Enter," Helga shouted.

In strode Sonas' Norse warrior, all bloodied and covered in muddy snow.

"Our clean floors," Sonas complained as he kicked off his boots. He ignored Helga and tore off his clothes. Would Helga go at all? For she stood watching until Ultan was naked and lifting Sonas into the barrel.

"Will we both fit?" Sonas asked, but he squeezed in front of her and doused himself with the warm water. He was big and there was barely any room for Sonas.

"Kiss me," he said and held her face as their mouths met. He tasted of mead and smelled of fresh air, and wet earth. She could feel his growing erection. There was no room to move, yet he stood and dragged her lower until she could submerge herself in the soothing, balmy water. He helped her wash and rinse her hair. His movements were caring, kind, and just perfect.

"What happened?" she asked and touched near a raw gash in his side.

He winced and sank lower to wash off the blood. "A boar got me before we killed the fiend. We'll eat well for a few days. But I might not be able for sex." He teased with a playful expression.

"Good." Sonas washed her face again. "I like feeling this clean. But I'm exhausted. We worked hard today with the rushes, and I aim to sleep tonight."

"In my bed?"

"Yes. The thoughts of you kept me going all day."

"All day?"

Sonas shrugged as water trickled down his chest. *How could she think of anything else? Was there some old inking under the hair?*

She inspected and rubbed over the faded swirls. "Will you let me rest if I go to your bed?"

"No," he said, kissed the base of her neck, and caressed down her back. "Maybe for a while...I will try."

He failed to lift her astride him. They laughed at the slippery and unsuccessful mating. Quickly, they climbed out and dried themselves and each other. He covered her in a large cloth and lifted her as if she were a feather. He strode naked to his bed and tossed her in behind the curtains. She heard him curse at Gruff, and then they both joined her in the furs.

She got out, plaited her damp hair, and commanded Gruff to leave them alone and by the time she managed everything, Ultan was sound asleep. *How handsome he was? How beautifully vulnerable despite his warrior ways? There was much she wanted to learn about him. Wanted to know about each scar on his rippled chest, broad back, and chunky thighs. What else might she do to please him? She would make him need and want her.*

She lay beside him and prayed they would always be like this together...and fate would be kind.

Chapter Thirteen

A Fool

Blood pumped into Ultan's cock. The sight of her sleeping was enough to torture a warrior's mind. Ultan tossed and turned. The more time he spent with Sonas, the more he cared. She bewitched him. The men mocked his feelings for a mere slave, and he spent the day tormented about his purpose for Sonas.

"What happened to the sacrifice for Odin? Your word to the gods means nothing?" Loki jeered the same statement, repeatedly, and in various ways throughout the day. "We marched back here in the snows for you to hump your Uppsala sacrifice. You are a doomed man, Ultan the Fearless. The gods will be cross."

Messing with promises to the gods was a dangerous thing. Loki was right, and he worried Ultan. Odin and Thor were toying with his emotions. Presenting him with a challenge. Dangling his love for Sonas and his oaths side by side. His men and the gods were laughing at his dilemma. Whatever was going to happen, he could not kill Sonas. For she was a light in the darkness of life. Yet their love distracted him from his ambitions and promises. Perhaps she was a test he was not mastering. His attention was not on his duty. He would have to change and had never been more afraid of anything in his life. These feelings for Sonas were unnaturally strong. What was he going to do? He was a coward in her presence. What if he couldn't protect or satisfy her? What if she left him? What if...? His oath was to use Sonas as a sacrifice... The gods were angry.

She slept. All his people slumbered, but there were other problems in Upvhal. Helga and Sonas did not mention Arden. Yet rumors were rife. Arden and two of the most trusted warriors were gone. They'd not turned up since Ultan returned. *Odd.* Although they were not close, there was a strong blood bond between them. Ultan's questions were unanswered, and their search parties and hunting found no trace of them. Arden could go for days, and sometimes weeks at a time, but never in the heart of winter. Despite the exhaustion, Ultan could not sleep.

If his father did not come back...would he be Upvhal's leader? How might Helga react? She would not stand aside too easily. There would be strife. Wives like Helga would not relinquish their power. Might she even try to kill him, Arden's son and successor? She possibly would. He was in danger in his own home.

He stroked his erection, remembering the previous nights. *Was there ever a passion like theirs before? For him? No.*

Sonas took all in stride. As if she knew he would love her and need their union. He saw her muttering prayers and offering smelling spices to the fire. The others said she was a healer, a potion maker...Almost a seer for her people. Loki also suggested she evoked spells to take Ultan's soul. Whatever Sonas was, there was a cleverness and power about her. These were reasons he both cared for and feared for the woman. She told fortunes for fun around the fire pit. He heard she made light of her talents, but she mentioned her secrets and some women were jealous of how Helga—

"You're awake?" she asked. Her hot breath tickled as she snuggled under his arm. A small hand gripped his cock. She pumped until the shaft was rock hard. The veins pulsed, and his desire was fiercer than ever. Red hair disappeared under the covers. He closed his eyes when a warm tongue licked his sack. *She took him into her mouth! And by the gods, he liked the sucking.*

The hot cavern cupped each ball. Her hand still pounded up and down. Then, suddenly, his tip was against her vicious tongue.

Fuck!

She sucked and sucked. Ultan lay there for a long while, letting her devour him. He thrust and moaned.

It was too good. Tight and wet. Better than pussy. He was going to erupt into her mouth.

He held her head, grabbed her hair, and drew her mouth down over his full length.

By the gods, he might die spilling his cock into her. He was on the edge of...he would...he could...give her his seed. To swallow.

"Argh!" he groaned and lifted the covers to watch. With a flop back on the pillows, his soul left him. *These feelings and what she did to him were too much. Just too much. He would have to stop her, stop whatever was between them, before he lost himself entirely.*

"Sleep," she whispered and turned her back. He curled in next to his goddess and tried to do as she commanded.

Since she came into his life, everything had changed. He was different. He was foolish and fearful instead of fearless. She would bring him power and glory. He was like a boy in love with an experienced woman. He was a toy in the hands of the gods. Even his men mocked him. Loki said she owned his cock. True. She did. But worse, she took his mind and heart, too. He'd not considered the spring raiding. There had been no trading in weeks…and he neglected to search for his father. Fool.

Then he caught her scent. The glorious aroma of his woman. She shivered as he nibbled her earlobe. His rough hand found a round and ready nipple. Her belly trembled as he found the triangle of wiry hair.

"Sleep," she said, but opened her legs. She was wet and her breathing was heavy.

She wanted his fingers. Kisses. He would give her anything. Everything. Turning her over onto her back, he kissed her hard on the mouth. Down and down he went. Over one breast and then the other. His fingers flicked past the nub between her folds. She held and rubbed herself with his hand.

"Just there," she explained. "There. Yes. I need you. Umm…yes."

He fumbled kisses on her neck and whispered into her ear, "My Sonas. My woman." Ultan rubbed on and waited for her femininity to respond. "You're mine. Always. Sonas with the flame colored hair and huge breasts."

He sensed her tense and slipped his thumb into her opening. The muscles puckered and accepted his probe, and he moaned on her cheek. "Always mine."

She strained and panted into his kissing mouth. "By my gods!" she cursed. "Dagda."

Then she was done. Sweat sat on her top lip as she bit in passion. *He wanted to bite her mouth, too.*

As he slept in a fitful slumber, his father came to him in a dream. The surrounding fog swirled out of the fjord's still waters. He spoke, but his voice was not his own. The pitch was high and woman-like, but his eyes burned with emotion and long, red flames darted from them when he said, "You must abandon the witch and follow your destiny. Sacrifice your love for her and give it to Odin. You must leave. Your life and my legacy depend on pleasing the gods. Go! Leave! Run from here, Ultan the Fearless."

When Ultan woke, his heart pounded and his mind turned over on itself like the waves of the ocean. The dream consumed him. "I'm sorry, my love," he whispered. "At first light, I must become Ultan the Fearless again."

A pain ripped across his heart. He was about to hurt himself, and couldn't stop. He should make his sacrifice.

"What do you mean?" Sonas asked.

"I'm lost."

"You're here with me."

"I don't know who I am anymore."

"What?"

He held his betraying heart. *He hadn't time for love. Hadn't space in his life for fear. The gods and his father demanded a sacrifice. This would have to happen. He would hurt them both, but there was one way to satisfy his father and the gods. They were forbidden.*

"I'm going to lose you. But I'm more worried about having you. When I'm with you, I'm afraid all the time." He couldn't look at her eyes. "I knew you were troublesome the moment I saw you."

"Trouble? I've done nothing wrong."

She was right, of course. This was all his fault. His

stupidity. He needed to fulfill oaths. Perhaps, then, the gods would return his father to Upvhal. Perhaps the test would be over. Somehow, they both would survive this. Maybe not together, but they would be alive. The gods would spare Sonas.

"I have work to do. Duties. Ambitions," he said.

She looked fearful. Tears. She was crying.

"And you gave your word to me," she sobbed.

"I did. You'll always be the only woman for me, Sonas."

"You regret your promise?"

"No," he lied. "I just...I must leave tomorrow. There'll be trouble if my father does not return."

Sonas held her mouth and pleaded with him through those beautiful eyes.

"If Arden does not appear soon," he continued. "I'll need to take charge. Then Helga will have me killed. Because she will believe I'll have her married off, murdered, or banished. I need to go. I cannot fight her with only three men. I'm in a weak position."

"Leave?" There was a sob. "And leave me? You cannot. You promised!"

He lay over her slight frame and pinned her on the bed.

She struggled for a moment. Then realized there was no point. She glared.

He took a deep breath. "I always knew you were to be my sacrifice. Now, I understand. I love you, Sonas. I do. From the moment I saw you. From the beginning, I should have known this was true *ást*. But I was a fool to think you were sent for a reason...I wanted to give your blood to Odin. Don't move. Listen to me! I took you from your home to give you to our priests in Uppsala.

They were supposed to slit your throat on an altar. I was to offer you as my powerful gift to the gods. But…I couldn't. I left you and abandoned the whole idea." He sniffed back tears, held her arms even tighter against the mattress, and nudged her legs apart with his knee. "I wanted to forget you and leave my fate in the hands of the gods, without a sacrifice. But when I was away, I thought only of you. I needed you in my bed. Under me. I ran back here and made a promise. But it is not right. I'm frightened. We are changing who I am. Do you hear me? I must sacrifice our *ást*. You are still my sacrifice. To remain Fearless and a great warrior, I must sacrifice my greatest *kærasta*. I will sacrifice… Us."

He wanted inside his woman, but she was clenching her thighs, squirming in his grasp and saying, "Get off me."

The dog growled and there was a sudden, searing pain in his leg. Blood spurted between his fingers.

Sonas screamed, "I'll try to hate you forever more, Ultan the Damned! I curse you! Yes, I will curse you to the end of time!"

Chapter Fourteen

Seasons Change

Sonas swore she wouldn't watch her love leave Upvhal. Yet she stood in the snow as his broad back blurred between the swaying trees. Ultan's sword glinted on the horizon while the storm raged and smothered Sonas' screams. Anger bubbled through her like never before. She raged into the gray skies. She cursed Ultan and her father repeatedly, and battered her breast and howled like a madwoman. Because of the fierce wind, her lover did not hear her torment.

"I will take my revenge. You'll pay for taking my freedom and my soul," she cried.

A slice with a sharp blade took her braid, and she dropped her red hair into the snow.

Thick drifts kept those sheltering in the longhouse captive for over a week. There was no sign of Arden. Helga declared herself the leader of Upvhal, and a peaceful calm descended while Sonas cried until there were no tears left.

People speculated Ultan and his men had possibly become lost in the bitterest blizzard in generations. Everyone feared for their safety, while Sonas swore she was not worried. She kept her mantra of curses going longer than the storm itself and frightened the other handmaidens and servants.

"I vow," she promised while drinking mead, "I vow to every god there is… I will have my revenge."

In those dark places in her mind, when she said prayers and spells, she included her increasing loathing for both her father and Ultan.

However, as much as she wished to kill the emotion, there in the corner of her broken heart lay a spark of hope. She could not quench the yearning for her Norse lover. No matter how hard she tried, she could curse him forevermore, but she would also love him.

Old Finnegan accepted her silence while they worked together. If Sonas were in Eire, they would have never allowed her in a forge. "I'm grateful," she said to Finnegan, "but my soul is in despair."

As the season turned, Finnegan sat her down beside the budding snowdrops and said, "We can choose to be miserable forever, or we can allow happiness to bud like these flowers."

While Sonas worked on the loom in the longhouse, she absorbed his wisdom. *She could have leaped from the ship on the journey to Upvhal, and could've thrown herself on the fire pit or from the walls of the fort, but she was stronger than she thought possible. Determined. To have her vengeance would take massive strength.*

Helga's hand rested on her shoulder. "You work too hard," she said. "Come, take your food. Sit with me."

As Sonas ate, she listened to the conversations. "I miss being your handmaiden," she admitted. "Those were happier days. I like my work, but sometimes I go for a whole day without speaking. Perhaps this is not good?"

"You've been grieving," Helga said. "As have I."

Sonas chuckled at the lie. Helga neither loved nor

cared for Arden. There was talk Helga murdered Arden (or had him killed). They said she buried him and his men in the far forest, or left for wild beasts during the snows. Instead of laughing at her mistress, Sonas smiled and replied, "Yes. This has been a harsh winter on us both."

"I think you must stop sleeping on the floor." Helga petted Gruff's head as he slunk in to steal bread. "No more lying with your dog. You deserve better. Did I not tell you before how special you are? Come to my bed. Yes. I think you should lie with me tonight."

Sonas choked. Even those outside the inner chamber knew that since Helga took charge, there were many men and women in her bed. Helga was a fine-looking woman, tall, lean, and full of womanly charms, and even without her power, she drew lovers to her.

"You will come?" Helga asked again with a flirting tilt of her blonde head. "Is there anyone else you wish to join us?"

Sonas was speechless.

"It is the right time for you to take a lover. Take me." Helga held Sonas' hand and kissed the palm. People gawped, and Sonas blushed. "I know you prefer men," Helga continued, "but I can do things to change your mind…if you let me."

Sonas gulped. *What on earth could she do? She adored Helga, but never really thought about being her bed fellow. Refusing her beloved leader would be difficult. What would be wise? Did she want this?*

As if reading her mind, Helga said, "Don't worry. You can refuse me. I know how awful being forced can be. I will wait until you choose to be with me."

"Thank you," Sonas said, for she meant total

gratitude. "You've always been kind. Always make me safe."

"And loved?" Helga let go of Sonas' fingers. "I would never have allowed Ultan to harm you. When he wanted to sacrifice you, I told him not to."

Sonas lowered her gaze and muttered, "Thank you."

"He's a fool. Like all men," Helga said with joy. "Their cock is useful. But only sometimes." She laughed loudly, and Sonas joined her. "Let us drink," Helga called to all those in the longhouse. "Let us drink to life, love, and humping! *Skål!*"

The roars vibrated through Sonas' bones.

Helga's lustful gaze never left Sonas. Over her full horn of mead, Helga asked, "Please, be mine? I only want you, Sonas. For the longest time, you are the only one. When the new season's contests and feasting finish tonight, you'll come to my bed? Say you'll forget the others who've hurt you and let me show you how wonderful life can be?"

They weren't alone, but she felt like they were…just her darling queen, waiting on a decision, from a lowly handmaiden… but she wasn't even that anymore.

Sonas could hardly breathe, but she needed to reply. "How can I refuse a gift?" She lifted her drink. "Let us believe in a happy future. *Skål!*"

Helga looked overjoyed. She even danced. The feasting became frenzied. Everyone was relieved to survive the dark days behind them. The atmosphere was hot. With Helga's interest, Sonas was light-headed and giddy. Also, impatient. The night's games lasted for longer than usual. Over the months in Upvhal, Helga's gaze was always on her, but had she truly known why? Helga always lusted after her body? Really?

Sonas shook her head but recalled the times at the bath barrel, and when Ultan took her the first night to his bed. Helga had watched them in the morning. *And it was pleasurable!* While in Eire, when Sonas lay with women in their group, they'd known how to kiss, knew where to touch, and how to make her feel unbearably beautiful. This kind of gentle kissing would be good.

Sonas wasn't lustful for many weeks, and now she imagined lying with her queen. These imaginings melted with memories of Ultan. The fire sparked and was hotter than usual. The mead tasted sweeter. Sonas drank more. The crowd roared with passion, writhing and wrestling men on the floor. Sweat and tension filled the air. When Helga touched the back of Sonas' neck and raised a suggestive eyebrow, Sonas leaped from her stool. "Yes," she said, panting. "Let's go to bed, my queen!"

Chapter Fifteen

Plans for Battle

The blizzard howled. Emotion clouded Ultan's vision and mind. Loki and the others hauled him to safety inside The Beggar's caves.

"We're almost halfway to Fiordland, but we'll have to wait here," Loki said.

They were angry. He would be too. Their lives were in danger in Upvhal and in even more peril trudging through the midst of a storm, and because of his foolishness.

"This too shall pass," Loki said. "We had to leave. At least, you had the sense not to lumber us with the Celt woman as well. Helga is a dangerous bitch, but she favors the wench. You shouldn't have trusted either of those witches. Arden, the poor fool, eh?"

"Helga thought she would have more time. She wasn't expecting us to arrive in Upvhal," Ultan said and wiped large chunks of snow off his furs. He stomped his boots nearer the cave's entrance. He said, "She wanted my father to take Sonas, or for him to give her a reason to have him killed. And she wanted me to condone what she did. But she did not have time for her plans, and he left Sonas alone."

"Are you only realizing now?" Loki crouched by a small bundle of kindling he kept in his traveling sack.

"Have we something to burn?"

"Nothing dry," one of his men replied. "Let's huddle."

Ultan did not want to sit. The winter would pass, but his life was upside down. He'd left his dead father, a vicious stepmother, and his greatest love in Upvhal. He was the biggest coward and fool.

****

His eldest son, Bjorn, strode from his home to meet them. The large flakes had stopped falling, but each step took time as they sank up to their frozen knees. Blond Bjorn was huge for seventeen. Freya was a tall woman, and Ultan was large, but Bjorn was going to be a giant. When his wonderful son greeted them with manly hugs, Ultan's bleeding thigh and hard heart felt slightly better.

Fiordland was bleak. Loki and the others insisted they were going the short distances to their dwellings. This meant he only had his two sons, a couple of servants, and the animals, to feast with. As the weather eased, with Ultan's terrible torment, Bjorn asked little. He knew his father well.

In the thaw, the homestead was even bleaker. In comparison to Upvhal, Fiordland was a hovel. Denial was one of his failings (and lack of modesty, too) perhaps. Yes, there was a good deep bay for his family's ships, but they lay at Helga's harbor. What did he have? Fuck all. Sonas was better off in Upvhal.

Bjorn lived up to the name of Fearless. As the days passed and they hunted together, Ultan could not have been prouder. His younger son, Ulrick, tended the goats, but he was a big part of Ultan's legacy, too. His twin boys would also add to his hoard of wealth through the generations, but Ultan also owned a secret amber mine.

Its stores were plentiful but hard to unearth. No one knew, and he rarely visited there.

At the turn of the season, Ultan's men returned to his settlement to plan. For the first time as a leader, Ultan did not have one. The dog bite oozed and was painful. He was used to battle wounds, but this was nasty and infected. Loki's wife helped and sent a healing poultice, but he needed to rest more, and of course, this was not something he did well.

"Helga cannot sit in Upvhal unhindered," Loki said and spat into the fire. "We followed you because you were to inherit. Fiordland is fine, but you are the ruler of Upvhal by right. If she wants war, then we'll give this to her. She killed Arden. Your father. Do you not want vengeance? And to take what is yours?"

"I want more than anything to survive and achieve my ambitions," Ultan replied. In the fire, he saw Sonas' smile and trusting eyes. Within the sparks, he heard her curses. "There has to be a better way," he said. "We'll have to fight my people, and I don't want this. Father would not approve either. There must be something else we can do?"

"You're worried about the handmaiden," Loki said and picked at his teeth with a knife. "She's bad luck. We've had nothing but trouble since the raid. She needs to be killed as soon as possible."

He knew better than to gasp or show shock, but fear rippled down his spine. Loki was dangerous. That was one reason Ultan kept him close. Loki never liked Sonas, and the others were nodding. They agreed with Loki. She was a liability. Shit!

"Your plan to sacrifice her was a good one, but we could make an altar in Upvhal instead. And cull her with the witch Helga. Save ourselves the journey to Uppsala. And take back what is yours."

"We'll need fighting men."

"If there is war or battle, the men will come," Loki said with a scary grin. "Some of those Celts we stole on the Irish raid are training up well. I've promised to pay them as berserkers."

"Can we trust them?" Ultan asked. "If Sonas is a danger, then surely trained killers are worse?"

"Some of them have found Norse women, and if they see gold or silver, they will fight. For me...for us."

Ultan stared at his childhood friend. "I know you took them as part of your hoard, but I didn't think you'd make a private army."

"That's six men," Loki said with a dismissive cough. "Not exactly a huge raiding party. They are ours. For the taking of Upvhal."

Ultan winced when he sat on the bench to eat his evening meal.

"The wound," Loki said and pointed with the blade. "The badness needs to be removed. And when we raid, we kill the hound as well. Then the wound will heal quicker."

Ultan ate in silence. Bjorn held his arm and grimaced.

"You've no other plan," Loki provoked at Ultan. "None. Look around you. No woman. Nothing. The Irish whore is full of badness and gave you a wound to take your leg as well. The bite has eaten your courage. We don't follow a coward, my friend. There's no time to waste."

Loki was mostly right. Finnegan mentioning Sonas' name meant happiness. When he was in her arms, he was content. Why had he not stayed there? He should have secured an alliance with Helga. Why had he run away? Because the great Ultan the Fearless was afraid. Worried about the gods' vengeance. Concerned about his dream and his father's words. But they were not from his voice. Perhaps, in fear, he had created another grave mistake. There could be no more cowardice. Loki was right.

"In the morning, we'll send out the call for men," Loki said and stabbed the blade into the wooden bench. "And then we take back what is yours."

"Yes," Ultan said and sat taller. "We go and take back what is mine. All my legacy will be fulfilled."

"*Skål!*" Loki shouted, and the men raised their drinks. "Battles lie ahead. And we've waited too long to see blood. Let us fight like never before. May the gods bring us riches, and if not, may they take us into their halls in Valhalla."

Ultan drank, but sniffed back emotion. "To victory or Valhalla," he roared. In a whisper, he muttered, "Forgive me, Sonas, my greatest love."

Chapter Sixteen

Danger comes to Upvhal

"My queen," Sonas moaned as Helga held her heaving breast and licked her nipple. The water in the small stream was fresh from the mountains and the rushes were tall. The other handmaidens were at a disinterested distance while Sonas washed Helga clean and kissed every place she could.

"You miss cock," Helga said as they dressed. "I know you do."

Sonas fixed on her new leather bodice and drew the lacing together. "Do you?" Sonas asked. *Ultan's cock was the only one she cared about.*

"No," Helga said. "I don't need men. Only you."

"Well, that's nice, but we need to get back. The season's tributes are coming."

"And you'll sit beside me?" Helga asked and waited for Sonas to dress. Sonas spent more time covering herself these days. Her garments were fine linen, with beautiful embroidery and silver brooches, and she took her time, and thanked the gods each time she put on each item. She cherished the small things these days because precious things disappeared.

"The people are worried," Sonas warned as she put on sturdy boots. "They believe Ultan will want to take Upvhal back. And soon. We need to make provisions and devise a plan."

Helga smirked in her wise way. She was a brave and admirable woman. "You pretend to hate him, but we both care far too much for Ultan the Fearless."

Sonas bent to kiss Helga's lips. "What are you hiding from me?" Sonas asked. "I sense there's something."

"We have more pressing problems. Our Jarl Dulca is coming to Upvhal. He sent word," Helga said as she dried the ends of her braids. Her beads rattled, and her bracelets shone in the sunshine. "I would imagine he means to either kill me or take me as one of his wives. Upvhal is a thriving port and village. He will want all. This is his right, as our jarl. I imagine he wants more power. You know I don't like being afraid."

Sonas sat on the damp moss-covered rock. "When?" she asked as her throat closed over with anxiety. "When will he come?"

"Maybe today or tomorrow, I'll need you to help me. We'll need to prove we are better allies than Ultan. Dulca will have his warriors with him. He's coming with his entire fleet. He'll claim Upvhal. There is nothing we can do to stop him, but we must survive. We must find a way to please his ego and remain intact."

"Aren't you afraid?" Sonas asked and took Helga's hand in her own. "You never show fear."

"Our fates are in the hands of the gods. I live with their will. I accept my fate."

"The people will fight for you, my queen."

"Farmers? A few handmaidens? The best men have pledged their allegiances to their jarl from when they were boys. I can't ask them to die. Because, Sonas, my love, I am not a queen."

"Will Dulca take you away?"

"He might just slit my throat?" Helga stood and held her hands aloft. "Dress me well. For it may be the last time you do."

The mood was somber in the longhouse since the people heard of the jarl's visit.

Old Finnegan's forge was busy making weapons, but this was a pointless exercise. When Sonas visited, he presented her with his best sword. "For the greatest handmaiden in Upvhal," he said and kissed Sonas softly on the mouth. "Don't use your weapon until there is a true battle." He strapped a sheath to Sonas' back and attached the blade. "This will end and we shall teach you how to fight in future battles."

Sonas nodded, but her eyes filled with worried tears.

"You are a Norse woman now," Finnegan said. "No crying."

The farmers did not linger. They left their tributes quickly. The atmosphere brimmed with haste and fear. There were no contests, drinking, or story-telling. Upvhal was in mourning. The air felt as if Helga had already died. Sonas couldn't bear the lamenting energy and stood praying to the stars. She cast all the spells. The rest was in the hands of the spirits. The night was dry when the warning horns from the lookouts sounded. Jarl Dulca's ships entered the bay.

Change sailed into Upvhal.

Sonas wore Helga's second-best cloak and sat to her right at the end of the fire pit. Helga was confident and defiant. She looked splendid in her finest garments and her jewels: bracelets, necklaces, rings, brooches, beads, a string of pearls, and a gold comb in her hair. Sonas knew where Helga buried the rest of her small hoard. But there would not be enough to pay off a jarl.

"You're the greatest woman I've ever known," Sonas said. "Let us drink to a bright future. Let us believe the gods will bring you even more power, my queen."

Helga was about to reply when Gruff barked. Menacing strangers with weapons and colorful shields marched into their home. The firelight flashed across their vicious battle-painted faces.

"I've come for Helga the Fearless," a man's voice called from the middle of the group. Sonas counted quickly. Twenty warriors, more coming. Thirty in total. Why was she looking for Ultan? Why did her heart leap at the thought he might be back? She was a fool.

The tallest and possibly the broadest man Sonas had ever seen stepped forward. He wore his wealth. Leather armor and furs that covered him to his thick neck. With a shaved head and a long, dark, high ponytail, he appeared larger.

Helga stood. Sonas did the same. "Welcome, Jarl Dulca," Helga said with confidence.

Sonas would have fallen upon his mercy immediately. She would have crawled, pleaded for her life, but Helga smiled. How brave she was. She faced death with dignity.

"There has been a tough winter," the jarl said. "Yet you have a fine home, fire, and family. Look at the wealth you have." His large arm extended as he surveyed all. "You are a genuine leader, Helga." He pointed with a thick finger. "You've done well."

Helga let out a sigh.

Sonas stared at their visitor. *Is he a friend or foe?*

"Today was our tribute day," Helga said. "I have good people. We have much to celebrate. Join us?"

Dulca bowed his head, accepting the invitation. Sonas still held her breath.

"Sonas. See to the feast for me," Helga ordered.

Then Dulca looked at Sonas.

He was close and might hear her thumping heart.

"Who is she?" he asked when he was just a few steps away. "A pretty, short-haired, red Celt?"

"This is Sonas," Helga said. "She is a handmaiden. My woman."

Sonas flinched at Helga's words and then glared. Charcoal blackened his eyelids. There was a long scar on his stubbled cheek and his temple was missing a chunk of skin (possibly bone) but his elaborate inking hid it well in the dim light.

"Ah," Dulca the Beast said, "I've heard of Sonas."

"You have?" Sonas replied with surprise.

Dulca smirked.

"I'll do as you've asked," Sonas said to Helga.

"Thank you," Helga urged.

If these men were guests, surely they would not harm their host. If Sonas hurried, they would be safe while the men were feasting.

"I hear Upvhal still has many boars to hunt," Dulca replied and marched past Sonas to sit in the seat left vacant. His scent was a powerful aroma of smoke, sweat, and blood.

When Sonas looked back over the fire pit, Helga was tiny compared to the beast of a man beside her. Sonas trembled and whispered a prayer to all the gods. *Helga would survive. She would save them all.*

Chapter Seventeen

The Beast

The scouts from Upvhal were back. Ultan sat by the path and waited, and he could see them coming. They ambled along. When they saw their leader, they quickened. He rested his leg from the perch on an old stump.

If his wound did not heal soon, his leg would be like a cut tree. He would not let Loki remove his limb until he lost all hope. A warrior needed legs. No matter how black his toes got, he would die before he lost a part of himself...again. He'd sacrificed enough.

"The news is bad," the men reported. "Jarl Dulca is in Upvhal. With his entire fleet."

How was he relieved and concerned at the same time?

"And Helga?" he asked. "Tell me, quickly."

"She is well. There is feasting and the jarl is giving his blessing to Helga's power seat in Upvhal. We came back before the jarl stopped us from leaving. He is demanding all fighting men swear loyalty to him again and stay to fight for him."

Ultan's breathing was heavy, and his forehead sweated from pain. "And my father?"

"No word. I'm sorry."

"What are the jarl's plans, then? To raid? From

where?"

"We heard he was going to send for his fighting men. They must come under his command at the next full moon."

"Come where? Upvhal?"

"Yes."

"Fuck."

Ultan limped back home and leaned on one of his scouts. "And Sonas?" he asked.

"She sits in your father's seat."

"Don't tell Loki," he warned his men. "He will know soon enough."

"Some say Sonas helped Helga murder Arden," the man said. "I don't believe the rumors. But she is a leader. They say she is even more powerful than Helga because Helga drinks and cares too much for Sonas. And I don't think Sonas feels the same way. We all heard she still pines for you, Ultan the Fearless."

Ultan covered his ears. His father's seat. Sonas in Helga's bed. He had lost her forever and sacrificed their love for nothing.

"What news is there?" Loki called out as he entered the longhouse.

"There'll be no raid. Jarl Dulca is in Upvhal," Ultan explained and bent his head to enter under the lintel of his home. "We'll have to fight under his flag instead."

Loki poked the spoon into the cauldron and turned the boiling vegetables over. The servants lingered, worried about the future and the meal.

"You'd be a fool..." Loki said.

"What choice do we have?" Ultan replied. "He's laid claim to Upvhal."

"He might leave Helga in charge there when he raids

and that would be the time to strike. Let us wait and see. There has been no command yet from Dulca. Things can change. And all you're worried about is you'll get back to your Celtic princess."

Ultan balled his fist. *He could thump Loki or challenge his behavior, but every part of him ached. His heart throbbed in agony. He was a coward and a fool. If truth be told, he hadn't sacrificed Sonas' love for greatness. He was too afraid. Too scared of the way she made him vulnerable. He'd left her to survive again without his protection. Sacrificed her safety for his selfishness. He did not deserve greatness or warrant health and happiness. He was not a true Norse, and the gods punished him. Ultan the Fearless! Pah!*

****

There was no seat for Sonas beside her queen. She sat with Gruff in the shadows. Just as she had all those moons ago when she observed Helga with the same awe and concern. The jarl's men were grateful for the food and ale. They were subdued and respectful. While the women filled their cups and plates, there were no lurid remarks. The musicians played old songs, but no one shouted the words. The fire was warm but did not flame or spark. A heavy air of danger lingered. All was eerily quiet. Gruff growled often. He sensed the tension, too. Sonas watched her beautiful queen.

If only she could use the sword strapped to her back.
If only she could protect them both.
If only she were more of a Norse.
If only she was Sonas the Fearless...

Helga's gaze found Sonas, and she beckoned for her to come to the top of the fire pit. *Would her legs carry her across the hall? Would she faint? She could not eat a bite. She was sick. Somehow she stood before The Beast. She was like a tribute. Perhaps she was?*

His smile was supposed to be pleasant, but Sonas shivered. Like a candle flickered, Dulca radiated power.

"Helga tells me you know Christians?" he said. Even his voice was firm. "Tell me about them."

"My father is one," Sonas admitted while she prayed silently to the pagan gods for strength and the right words. "I've vowed to take his breath and send him to his heaven. He sold me. I hate Christians."

"She is like fire," Dulca said to Helga. "You're right, Helga. To get at your father's body would mean you somehow raid your country, Sonas the Celt? Would you use the fine sword at your back?" he asked. His tone was curious and did not mock her.

"I'm not a shield maiden. Not yet," she muttered.

"Sonas is a healer, a weaver, and a metalworker. She has power over everything she touches," Helga said, pride in her features. "People love her. I love her."

Dulca supped from his cup before speaking. "I hear Ultan the Fearless cares for her, too. Yet, he left Upvhal. Abandoned her here."

Helga's expression told Sonas she did not provide the jarl with the information.

"I'll send Ultan the Fearless to Valhalla as well," Sonas said. "I was to be his sacrifice. Then, he changed his mind and vowed to protect me. Vowed I would be his woman. He broke his word. He will pay for his betrayal."

"And…you cursed him," Dulca said, sitting back into the chair. "You gave him a new name. Ultan the Damned. You're a dangerous woman, Sonas the Celt. What might you call me?" He licked the honey from his finger. "If I said you could not seek vengeance because you were to be my sacrifice, what would you say, Sonas the Celt?"

Sonas paled. She was weak as water. Helga smiled, and she would not beg or crawl. Sonas was like Helga, her queen. The Beast waited for her answer.

"A man such as you would not need to sacrifice good women," Sonas replied as her voice caught in her throat. "Real men, with actual power, would be more clever than a simple warrior. You are a great man, and you have heard of me. Therefore, I would suggest I bring more power to you alive."

Helga's breathing sounded worried. Dulca picked a dried fruit from the bowl and ate. A knife could cut the air.

"You've answered well," Dulca said. "Now, what do you call me? I bet you have decided on my title. Tell me, what is my new name?"

"I'll need something in return," Sonas replied as her cheeks pounded. "Promise me…Helga can keep power in Upvhal."

"You do not ask for your own life?" he asked, sitting forward. "And you trust a Norse's word?"

"I must."

"Helga's leadership is safe. Tell me what you call me," he said with a huge grin. "What does beautiful Sonas the Celt think of her jarl?"

Sonas took a deep breath and dug fingernails into her palm. "You are Dulca the Beast," she said. "Dulca the Ugly Beast."

Chapter Eighteen

The Jarl's Allies

The jarl's commands to come to Upvhal reached Fiordland. However, a fever took Ultan, and he languished in his bed. With delirium, he called out for Sonas both day and night. Bjorn guarded his injured leg from Loki and secretly sent one of the trusted scouts back to Upvhal.

"The amber," Ultan muttered.

"I'll not tell a soul. Please be quiet, Father," Bjorn whispered. "All is good. You're safe. I've sent for the healer. Loki and the men have left. They'll not fight for Jarl Dulca. Did you hear me?"

Ultan listened, but his mind was not his own. All that remained was Sonas: her image, her smile, her smell. He was lost. His sacrifice was not enough. Odin wanted him to die in his bed and he would not go to Valhalla.

****

All was quiet when Sonas opened her sleepy eyes. Chinks of the dawn found their way into the inner chamber as she automatically rolled over to hug Helga. She was sitting propped up on the feathered pillows.

"He liked your name for him," she said. "Thank the gods. You showed no fear. Good. I thought he'd tell us more about what our fate might be. He didn't come all this way for a small feast..."

"He promised your safety," Sonas said, stretching.

"Humph!"

"You're welcome," Sonas replied with a wry smile. "I could've asked for his favor instead."

Helga reached out for her in the dim morning light. "I know. Come here."

Their kisses were always delicate and took Sonas away from her troubles. They also descended onto skin and more intimate places. They spent hours on their love-making, but mornings were deliciously frenzied.

"Let me eat your pussy," Helga ordered, pushing Sonas back onto the mattress. "Open those legs for your queen."

Sonas was tired, but obeyed. Helga was an expert at pleasuring her. Her touch was soft until she needed to be probing and insistent. "Give me yours," Sonas asked, but Helga was already moving her crotch level with Sonas' mouth. "You're wet," Sonas said, parting Helga's folds to lick, nibble, and suck. Their moans mounted. "Sit more on my face. Take me with your fingers. Put them in deeper. Faster. Like that, yes." Sonas liked to talk. Helga always listened. "I'm going to come against your tongue. Flick over…ah…good. Too nice."

Sonas sensed Helga's familiar peak approaching, too, and she sucked on her clit and fingered her. She stopped only to say, "I'm going to come, but you must come first."

Helga panted and just as Sonas peaked, Helga clenched her thighs and inner muscles and came hard against Sonas' mouth. They lay there as usual, savoring the feelings.

Then, Gruff growled.

"Who's there?" Sonas called. The chamber was

empty. (Or should have been). The doors were still closed.

A male figure stood outside the curtains around Ultan's old bed. In two heartbeats, Sonas recognized Jarl Dulca. The Beast.

"You," Sonas said and covered herself in fur as best she could.

Dulca was naked, huge, and erect. "The Ugly Beast is awake," he said and rubbed his cock.

Helga froze to the spot. For the first time, she looked scared.

"I came to speak with you both last night. But the dog was on guard."

Sonas stared at the size of the rigid, long, thick snake nestled in a large crop of hair, between huge muscular thighs. The massive cock wavered over his impressive sack as he walked closer still. *Would he even fit inside a woman?*

He sat on the edge, and Helga's wooden bed cracked under his weight. The inked markings on his arms and chest rippled under a layer of dark hair. He leaned an elbow farther onto the mattress. Every inch of him was lean, and the helmet on his cock was red and dewy.

"You're quiet, Helga, my queen," Dulca teased.

Helga was pale. She held Sonas' cold hand.

"Don't be afraid," Dulca said. "I liked what I saw and heard. Both last night and this morning were impressive. I have a proposal."

Sonas moved, but a large hand stopped her from leaving.

"I have a suggestion for you both," Dulca said. "You'll guard my interests here in Upvhal. Together. You're a good team."

"Why do I think there is a catch?" Sonas asked.

Helga was still silent.

"There isn't one. You've not challenged me. There's no need for me to remove you from Upvhal. Ultan was a concern, but he is usurped. I am grateful. The people here are content. I can see why."

Helga shook her head and bit her lip. Like Sonas, she was waiting for the bad news.

"The only problem is I've listened to you both and I'm horny. Have you good whores in Upvhal?"

Sonas laughed out of nervousness. Helga said nothing.

"Or maybe I should just take more wives?" Dulca suggested and tugged on his cock. "Sonas, Helga, would you let me into your bed? Would you take me as a husband?"

He isn't serious? He can't be. Helga will not agree. Would she? Had they a choice?

"Ah Sonas, we know what he wants," Helga said and placed her hand over Dulca's. "I've always wanted to be a jarl's wife," she said as she stroked the thick-veined monster in their joint grasp. Dulca lay back farther into the bed and gripped Sonas' leg while he groaned in desire.

"Both of us? You want us both?" Sonas asked. "You need two more wives?"

"Why not?" Dulca said between loud moans from Helga's magic touch.

"Does the thing even fit inside a woman?" Sonas asked in all seriousness. "The biggest I've ever seen."

He liked praise because he bucked and thrust into Helga's fists. "I want you both," he said before crying out and spurting a stream of semen onto his heaving belly. "Say you agree."

Chapter Nineteen

Storms over Upvhal

The healer rarely entered the longhouse. She wore raven feathers, and when she walked, she rattled the bones of her predecessors stitched to a cloak. The smell and sight of her were hard to miss, and a dirty and dyed fingertip beckoned Sonas to the doorway.

"I'll teach you sword skills," Dulca said to Sonas as he ate the food his men prepared. "Are you listening to me? What's the matter? Why the worried face?"

"She is the healer. I must go to her."

"What do you want from the witch?" Dulca squinted toward the door.

"We won't be buying poison for our husband," Sonas said with a chuckle. "Let me talk to her."

"Bring her here," Dulca suggested as he touched Sonas' arm. "I want to hear why she has come."

Since Dulca joined them in bed, he was less frightening. But Helga was still wary, and left to bathe with the handmaidens in the stream.

Why was the Beast fascinating? What kind of human was the size of a god? What type of man held such power? He was fierce in battle, but there were many tales of his kindness to the sick and those less fortunate. His warriors and their families all sang of his greatness. He ruled with a mixture of fear and respect.

"I need the jarl's permission to leave Upvhal," the healer said and gazed at the floor in a low bow before them all.

"To go where?" Dulca asked.

"Someone needs me?"

"Who? Someone important?"

She did not want to answer, and the bones on her cloak shook as she left.

"Stop her," Dulca ordered.

The healer turned to answer before they manhandled her. "Ultan the Fearless is injured and gravely ill. His son Bjorn sent for me."

Sonas blurted out, "Ultan? Sick? For how long?"

"I don't know. Too long. I must go."

"Yes," Sonas said with tears in her eyes. "My jarl will agree?"

Dulca took spoonfuls of his porridge and scratched at his beard. "Go," he said to the healer. "A weaker warrior might be jealous of his wife's concern for another man," he continued to Sonas. "Sit, beautiful. Remove the weapon you cannot wield yet and tell me about your masters and what happened here."

"There's nothing to tell," Sonas replied. "Arden disappeared and Ultan left in the middle of the storm, muttering something about Helga murdering him, too. Weak fool."

Dulca ate and asked for another bowl. "You still care for him," he said. "I can hear this in your voice. Sit."

Sonas threw her leg over the bench, and Dulca encouraged her to sit in his lap. He held her hair to speak into her ear. He yanked tighter, and her scalp hurt. "I ask only one thing of you, my beautiful Celt. One thing."

Sonas nodded.

His full fist wrapped around her hair, tight to her aching scalp. He spoke again. "I ask you to respect me. Not like a servant does their master. Not like an obedient slave. I ask you to respect me as a man, as a husband, and as an equal. Promise me you will tell me the truth...always. No matter what. I want the truth from you. Understand?"

"What a big ask," Sonas said and gritted her teeth in defiance. "Men don't always want the truth."

"I do," Dulca said and released his grip slightly. "I know you watch people. You guess what they are thinking. I do this, too. But I don't always know everything. You see me as a beast. An ugly one. You're correct. But I am also a jarl, and no one tells me the truth. I hear lies all the time. I am no fool, but I get tired, and miss things. Can I depend on you?"

"You won't sacrifice me then?" Sonas asked and stared into his charcoal-covered eyes. Without waiting for an answer, she said, "Can I start immediately? And tell my husband he stinks like the beast he is."

Dulca laughed and threw his new porridge bowl away. Then he nuzzled Sonas' neck and kissed her skin lightly. "You vixen," he whispered. "Promise me. The truth. Always."

"I shall always love Ultan the Fearless," Sonas said and didn't care who heard. "But...I will respect my jarl Dulca and tell him the truth. This is my vow."

"Stay here next to me," Dulca said gently and unfurled his grip on her hair. He touched the small of her back. "I promise to bathe later." He sniffed his fingers. "You smell nice, though. Stay and tell me what you know of your jarl?"

"You want more of the truth?" Sonas started with a

wry smile. "They say you are a vicious warrior but rule well. With fairness."

"Good," Dulca said. "I've been told you have a strange hold over men. Helga seems bewitched, too. Am I to be next?"

"Perhaps."

Dulca laughed and slapped Sonas' thigh. "I think you're too late, my beautiful Celt. I am smitten. However, if you love another, I may have to seduce you."

Sonas held her tongue, and her heart leaped in her chest. *What was to become of her in Upvhal?*

She was surprisingly comfortable against the bulk of the jarl. He leaned his heavy arms over her shoulders. Despite the smell of his furs and unwashed armpits, when she lay back against his broad chest and sat between his massive thighs—*there was a twinge of desire. He wanted a wife. Her? She would be his equal. He was a beast. A giant. But he held power and returned respect. He was fearsome, and the mixture of fear and intrigue was like a drug.*

While in the middle of a conversation with one of his warriors, he stopped and asked, "What do you think, Sonas?"

"What?" she stammered. "I wasn't listening."

"Why? What are thinking about?"

Sonas blushed, and the men chuckled.

"Tell me," he said, grabbing one of her breasts.

She was shocked into speaking. "The truth is…I'm still thinking about your enormous cock."

The men laughed…and Dulca howled. Sonas joined them.

The merriment ended with Helga's return. "The sky

is dark as dried cow's blood. There is a bad storm coming," she said with anger. Thunder sounded around the longhouse. "Thor and I are desperately unhappy."

Chapter Twenty

Taming The Beast

"To be a legendary warrior, a man needs his legs," Ultan complained and rubbed the thick bandage. "Odin himself has blessed me. The pain is easing, the swelling, too."

Bjorn gnawed on a chicken bone. Grease dripped from his fuzzy chin. "I've been worried for days," he murmured. "The healer eats like a cow. We're glad to see the back of her."

"You paid her for my care?"

"In amber. She drove a hard bargain, but when you were at the doors of death, I gave in to her demands."

"How much?"

"No matter. We'll have plenty more."

"No one else knows about the mine?" Ultan asked and held his breath.

"Of course not."

"You're a dutiful son. Where's Ulrick?"

"In the forest. Setting snares."

"I thank the gods. I am healing, and I still have my wealth. My sons. The amber," Ultan said. "I'll make offerings in gratitude when I'm better."

"Our scout didn't return," Bjorn added. "You might make a plea to Helga for his safety. If we're not too late. The healer said she must ask special permission to leave

Upvhal. She told him you were sick. At least he'll know why we did not come to honor his call for fighters."

"Did she say where they were going to raid?" Ultan asked, his interest perked. "If we rally to his cry, we can replace our hoard. Even if we must fight under Dulca's flag…"

"There's no word about him."

"Is he still in Upvhal?"

"As far as we know," Bjorn said. "Even if he isn't, if we try to take Upvhal back, he'll return."

Ultan stumbled up and limped around. "The healer knows Sonas," he said thoughtfully. "Did she mention how she is?"

"Of course. Sonas is the talk of Upvhal!"

"Why?"

"From lying with the dogs on the floor, she's carrying the best sword, and is Helga's woman, and she was in the company of the jarl when the healer entered the longhouse. There's an alliance forming there. For sure."

"What kind? What do you mean?"

"They were sitting, eating, and laughing together."

"Shit."

What had he done? The sacrifice of losing Sonas was too great. His heart would never cope with the torment. Hearing of her surviving without him was good, but also painful. He would not cry in front of his son. Her fate was not in his hands anymore. There was nothing to be done. All was lost.

"Once you rest, what's the plan?" Bjorn asked.

"We go to Upvhal for the gathering. We follow our jarl's call. What else can we do?"

"And Helga?"

"We wait for our revenge. All is her doing. She has taken everything. My father. Sonas. My birthright. Loki and the men left us because of her. I'll make her pay in gold, blood, and tears. By Odin, I will."

****

Sonas swung her sword. When the metal clashed with Dulca's blade, the shockwaves were unbearable, and she dropped her own. The mud sucked her boots and the heavy weapon. She dug both out while Dulca laughed.

"Stop mocking me," she complained. "You're like a wall of hairy muscle with arms. How am I to fight you? Standing on tiptoes, I'm still not up to your shoulder. Pick a smaller man for me to practice with."

"No," he said in a good-humored tone. "I want to. Looking at you sweat and feeling your anger hardens my cock."

"My sword is too small as well," Sonas said. "Made of a strong metal, but the weapon is tiny compared to yours. I am poking at you with a sewing needle."

"No more moaning. Try the moves again," Dulca said and braced himself for the motions he had suggested earlier. "And I like how you look in tight leather armor. This is fun."

"Huh!" Sonas roared and battled with The Beast. *I am getting the hang of his movements.* But then she lost her balance and slipped over, falling head-first onto the wet ground.

Dulca lifted her from the waist as if she were a twig. "Again," he called. True to his word, they practiced until dark. They dripped with sweat and mud, and every part of Sonas ached.

"A cool bathing barrel for me and one for your

mistress," Dulca ordered the servants. "Then we'll all eat together. Helga, too."

Sonas ignored the naked Beast as he jumped into his barrel with a splash. Her hair had grown slightly longer, and she tied it, and dropped her robe. The cold water shocked, but eased her bruises and strained limbs.

"Thank you for today," she said while she washed her armpits.

"You have stamina," he praised. "My servants have given us privacy, but now I must wash myself. Hmm?"

Sonas laughed and threw him a bar of scented soap. "In your past, you must have washed your arse?"

"I must have done," he replied with a smirk. "But I don't remember."

"Did a sword make the mark on your head?" Sonas asked and pointed to his scar. "How did you survive? Even I know a blow there can be fatal. There's a whole chunk missing."

"I was hot in battle. My first. I am a big target and covered in battle scars. And before you say I'm not telling you the truth, the rumors are wrong. The injury was not from one of my wives."

She smiled. *He had a knack for comedy. He was good company. Perhaps the name she gave him was a hasty one.*

"I'm glad to hear this," Sonas said. "How many do you have? I meant how many wives…not holes in your head."

"You've not heard then?" Dulca replied with a grin. "No…"

"The legend is…I murder them," he said. "Don't worry, I'm joking. All but one died of natural causes."

"And the poor soul? What did she die of?" Sonas

asked, her tone high and concerned.

"She couldn't handle my cock," he said and chuckled. "Your face, Celt. My last wife, Astrid, is not dead. When I left, she was alive. She is one hard, bitter little bitch. But I admire her. Like Helga, she rules well."

"What will they think of each other? What will Astrid think of me?"

"You'll never see her. There's no need to poke a poisonous snake."

"Where will you be? With Astrid? Or with us?" Sonas asked, and instantly regretted her nosiness.

"Neither. A Norse must raid. I've called for the warriors to unite."

"I heard."

"Ultan the Fearless will return to Upvhal?"

Sonas shrugged, trying to hold in her anger, her fears, and her tears.

"I cannot let you kill him," Dulca said. "If he pledges loyalty to me, I must give him my protection. And I need his sword and men. Your revenge will have to wait. However, to make up for the disappointment, I have a different proposal for you, my beautiful Celt…"

Chapter Twenty-One

Sailing On

"What do you mean she left with Dulca?" Ultan asked. His neck veins protruded, and his forehead wrinkled in disgust. "And I'm supposed to go to England? With these scrawny remnants he left behind?"

"He thought you'd have Loki and your men," Helga said with her annoying smirk. She sat in Ultan's seat, and the newest young handmaiden held her hand. Like they were a mating couple. The absolute cheek. He should kill all of them. But Helga was who he called mother.

"I'm Dulca's wife," Helga explained. "As is Sonas. He took her away with him to kill her father. Dulca will no doubt have more plans for her, but his monumental cock blinds her—" Helga stopped to let the statement linger. "—I tried to stop her, but he is a jarl, and he wanted her. What could I do? The desire between them must be good. Even though I did not see them hump, I watched him take her from me. I've no tears left."

"Are you drunk?" Ultan asked.

"I am," Helga slurred. "Since they left yesterday."

Ultan cursed. Bjorn frowned at him to stay quiet.

"Good to see you, big Bjorn," Helga said.

"He's a wise son," Ultan praised. "He thinks you would never harm me."

Helga's eyes widened and then squinted. "Sonas

said you thought I would take your life. You fool, I did nothing to Arden and would never harm his sons. You have half brothers and cousins here who love you. Do you think they would let me harm Ultan the Fearless?"

Ultan shook his tired head, but he did not agree. He could never trust Helga. Something deep inside him told him not to.

"Anyhow, the jarl said you were to be spared," Helga said and hiccupped. "And we must obey our men." The scoff she let out sent her handmaidens into giggles.

"We all have a burden we don't want," Ultan said.

"All except Sonas," Helga replied. "She came out of this well."

Ultan grinned, but looked for Bjorn to speak, and he did. "Father got injured. He was gravely ill."

"We heard. Sonas did not seem too bothered by the news."

Ultan's stomach turned over. He longed to sit and ease his leg, but he waited to be welcomed into the home that was rightfully his own. *He would to hold his temper. May the gods Eir and Baldr send patience and mercy, for he was going to crumble.*

"You're improved though? And alive? I'm glad," Helga said. "What happened to you?"

"A dog bite," Bjorn replied.

"Pah! She took the traitorous beast with her," Helga snarled. "He was my dog. She stole my hound, my heart, my cunt…She took them all. Just like she took everything from you, Ultan the Fearless."

"She took your animal?" Bjorn asked.

"He's not mine anymore. The hound fell to her heel, like us all," Helga said with a slight sniff and added, "Will you both sail for Dulca?"

"Bjorn is too young," Ultan said. "And I'm not fit."

"You wish to stay in Upvhal, then?" Helga asked and closed one eye in suspicion. "When Dulca returns and you do not abide by his wishes, will you be able for the consequences?"

"Will you?" Ultan asked and gestured toward the handmaiden, who clutched Helga's hand. Helga released the hold and smirked in resignation.

"I'll deal with Dulca," Ultan said with some confidence. "And I've plans for his new wife."

Helga slurped from the large cup, slapped the arm of her power seat, and asked, "And what do you aim to do with me?"

If only he could say what he wanted. If only he could...

****

Sonas tingled at the memories of their bed. Dulca grinned down, and she rested against him in the boat's prow. The hooked dragon's head loomed above them and strained into the waves.

She was going home as the wife of a powerful man. How?

"I'm thinking of last night, too," Dulca said, and his voice carried on the wind.

"There's no need to shout," Sonas replied and glanced at those rowing, and added, "I think your mind might be foggy from the ale."

Dulca kissed the top of her head and held her shoulders.

He was a considerate man. Attentive. Did she care for him? Trust him? She wasn't certain. Whatever type of beast he was, Dulca captained a vessel well, and the organized atmosphere was calm and pleasant. The men were good-humored. The weather was sensible for travel and the future was bright.

"You look content, wife," Dulca said as the sun dipped onto the horizon. "You've smiled most of the day."

"I want to thank you, husband. My last voyage was very different."

"Of course, you were Ultan's slave," Dulca said and yanked her hair and head back until his mouth met hers. There was no anger, yet the touch was nice and rough. His lips almost touched hers, but he stopped, and she yearned for his kiss. She strained upward to greet the passion. He eased back; teasing, smiling. "And you're a jarl's wife," he said and plundered his tongue into her parting lips, taking her breath. She clung to his furs. He broke free and was breathless. "I thought I might have persuaded you to be mine, and I am going to make a show of myself here in front of the men," he said and rearranged his crotch.

Sonas cupped his balls in her palm. The enormous Norse moaned and closed his eyes as she smoothed down the long length of his hardening cock. The men rowed with their backs to them. The others were asleep. Secretly, Sonas loosened his belt and delved into the warmth. He was too large to pull on at that angle, but she held him, and he pulsed in her grip. Dulca hugged her. Bending down, he groaned into her ear as she continued her massage.

"Watching you eat Helga's pussy drove me wild," he muttered. "And then…when she let me lick hers, the juices of her cunt tasted sweet. Yours will be like honey. And I still can feel how I was sucked by your pretty mouth."

Sonas moaned in agreement and rubbed on. She liked when he talked and wanted more.

"I'm going to spurt. Stop. I cannot let you…" Their kisses muffled his protests and pleasure. Sonas stopped her fumbling in his trousers, but only when he was peaking. She slipped out her hand just as suddenly as she'd slipped in. Dulca's frustration was obvious in his features; his jaw clenched, mouth half open, brow furrowed. "You're a dirty whore," he cursed, but there was a desire in those dark eyes. "I warn you when I get you ashore…" he said through gritted teeth, "I promise you, my beautiful Celt, I'm finally going to ride you raw."

Chapter Twenty-Two

Three or More

"Did they fuck in my bed?" Ultan asked a servant. "I'll want new coverings."

Bjorn grunted a long noise in his throat.

"What?" Ultan asked, his voice high with annoyance.

"Will we be able to sleep anyhow?" his son asked and pointed to the naked men and women strewn across Helga's bed. All the bodies slept after taking some of the magic mushroom crop. "What a busy place," Bjorn continued. "I might join them."

"You sound hopeful," Ultan teased. "What would your mother say?"

"She's bedding her cousin, Jarl Borg."

"Are you sure?"

"I am."

"Still. You're too young."

"I'm not," Bjorn said and elbowed his father to keep his voice lower. "Look at her on the end. Beautiful. Would you stop me from enjoying her?"

"No," Ultan said with a chuckle, for Bjorn was already removing his boots and clothes. "I'll get some air."

Ultan turned a blind eye as Bjorn set to work upon the woman. He did, however, notice the pert breasts and slender legs as Bjorn snuggled in next to her.

"How nice to be young and virile," Ultan muttered and trailed his sore leg after him into the great hall.

The noise when he entered the hall was from the preparations for the evening meal. There was to be a feast for their return, after all.

Helga sat at the top of the fire pit. She too was half-asleep—caught in a haze of grief Ultan recognized.

Outside, the evening was fresh. The searing pain in his leg had improved to a dull ache, and he visited Finnegan's forge. The door was ajar.

"Finnegan, you old bastard," he said. "Are you here?"

The fire smoldered, the scent of sawdust and molten metal filled the air. There was a noise behind the tall workbenches. Ultan stood stock still when he spied Helga's main handmaiden on her knees and Finnegan's bare arse pumping into her from behind. *They were like dogs. Noisy. Everywhere, people were fucking. Could he leave without disturbing them? Did he want to?*

If he left, he would alert the couple, and yet, if he stayed, he would hear the slapping of flesh on flesh, smell the musk in the air, and see her buck back in a frenzied rhythm to match Finnegan's thrusts.

Ultan's groin throbbed as he covered his face. But there was too great a temptation, and he peeked between his fingers.

They hadn't noticed him. He'd just wait a minute. Any man in his position would do the same. There was nothing else for him to do.

The woman was a shield maiden; her leg muscles pronounced, her dress open, her breasts bouncing and unharnessed. Finnegan's coarse fingers dug deep into those smooth, lean thighs as he continued pumping. Old Finnegan had staying power, for her groans were loud and long. *Could I fuck like him? He doubted his erection would last very long because the woman cursed and roared. She thrilled him too much. He would surely come, if he felt her skin, and sank his tip into the moist tunnel...*

"Fuck me. Fuck me. More. Harder," she urged.

Ultan groped his big bulge and squeezed on his hard cock.

Finnegan sounded like he was almost done, but she was furiously rubbing between her legs warning him, "Don't you dare stop. I need you to give me more. More!"

Ultan's breath caught in his chest as he snuck a trembling hand between his clothes. With a long sigh his palm reached his erection. Just as he pumped over the throbbing veins and flicked a thumb over his moistening tip, Finnegan came in a roar, and heaved out his seed over the woman's back.

Her anger was sudden and furious as Finnegan withdrew. "You cannot be finished?" she shouted at Finnegan. Wheeling around, she saw Ultan immediately. No longer sounding cross, she seductively asked, "How long have you been there?"

"Long enough," Ultan replied and then said to his friend, "I'm sorry, I didn't mean to..."

"I know you have a bad leg but is your cock working?" the shield maiden asked. "I need to come. Take whatever you're holding out of those britches and let me see if you will do."

Did Finnegan care she was looking for another man? He was indifferent.

107

With his cock clothed, Finnegan stood against the bench and folded his arms. "If you want her, she's all yours," he said.

"Show me," she shouted and Ultan awoke from his uncertainty. "Now."

Ultan dropped his trousers and bared his erection. While he fisted, he mouthed a prayer to Odin. *Can I satisfy her? She was attractive, but she was not Sonas. If he thought of loyalty, he would soften. Those breasts were plump and the small nipples a nice pink. Ripe for a suck. He'd do damage if she let him.*

Ultan stroked himself a few times to show eagerness and ignored Finnegan's stares. She got off her knees and leaned over the workbench beside Finnegan without hesitation. She spread her cheeks and showed Ultan all. "Take me. And hurry up," she said.

"Any man would," Ultan said to Finnegan as he placed his tip at her opening. "She's wet and wants me."

"Yes. She does," Finnegan said matter-of-factly.

Ultan stuck his cock into the wetness and moaned as the sensation took over. His thigh shot pain through him as he thrust, but he didn't stop his stride. Finnegan left the bench with a cough. *He was watching. And Ultan liked an audience. She was not Sonas, but she was the next best thing. A hot whore would do, and she liked his cock. He could hear shouted instructions.*

She rubbed her nub. Those vicious fingers clashed against him as he rode into the gripping hole. He lifted one of her legs from the floor a little and sunk in deeper.

"Yes!" she roared. "There. I'm coming. Up in there is too good. There. Yes. Take me, Ultan the Fearless."

He drowned in a tortured pleasure. His vision blurred and his heart thumped. *He was alive and fucking a beautiful woman. There was nothing better! Unless she was Sonas. But Sonas abandoned him. And there was a different woman who wanted his cock and expected nothing. She just wanted him. If he imagined Sonas...the fuck would be even better. He would erupt. He would give in. She was his love, his Sonas, his happiness. Then, the arse and hole he was fucking clenched over his heaving cock. He couldn't help coming and wouldn't stop emptying himself as she finally let go. She shuddered under him. He did this. He gave her a great fuck.*

"There, Sonas," he said aloud and slapped flesh while he took out his limp cock out. "You've missed me, your best lover."

Ultan realized his mistake.

"I've had better," the shield maiden said and then she kissed Finnegan with tongue. "Sometimes an older cock is the best of all."

Chapter Twenty-Three

Hibernian Promise

The Norse longship bobbed about in the sunshine. Sonas did not haul oars or bail out water. The butterflies in her tummy were from anticipation, and the wash of the waves sounded like joyful music calling her home. She quivered despite a determined grasp on the wet ropes and her new husband's waist.

How would she be received by her kin now that she was a powerful woman? Whatever happened, one thing was certain: her treacherous father would pay for selling her for a pittance to a Norse raider. He could have ruined her, but she was returning as a jarl's wife. A queen of sorts. A full turn of the seasons brought change into her life. Was she grateful for Ultan the Fearless? Where was he? Was he dead from whatever the healer was called to fix? No. He survived. She felt him in her bones. He yearned for her as much as she longed for him. How could she still have feelings for the cowardly fool who called himself "fearless"?

Dulca's bulk saved Sonas from the biggest of the waves. "Land-ho," he hollered and pointed at squawking seagulls overhead as he shook salt water from his hair and furs. "This was where I ordered Ultan to come for those raids. If he did as he was told, this is your homeland, my beautiful Celt. Do you recognize this place?"

"No," Sonas said. "I rarely looked inland from a ship. Wait, he might be at the O'Neill castle on the cliff."

Dulca shielded his eyes from the glare of the light on water, and his expression turned to greed.

He liked what he saw. Lusted for the supposed wealth. Had Ultan the Fearless made a similar face when he came close? Probably. What would Dulca do? Helga warned Sonas. Dulca would not simply sail her home and leave. He was hatching a plan, but what? Could she dare think...

"The castle is just a ruin. My father is useless," Sonas added. "He's an O'Neill, but he's not a leader...like you."

Dulca chuckled, yet didn't take his eyes off the prize. "Farmland?" he mused aloud. "Fishing boats, too, and you say they are Christian. Gold. Gold. Gold."

"Any riches are long gone. The monks or holy men left to go south," Sonas said. "Dulca, you promised me there would be no raiding of my people."

"My word is my vow. I have plans, though. What do you call this place?"

"Part of Tyrconnell, a small port called Bun an Phobail, lies around the headland...there."

"What kind of welcome will we get?" Dulca asked and rested his hand on the head of his ax nestled into his belt.

"Hard to say," Sonas replied. "I doubt there'll be much resistance. My father gives Vikings what they ask for, including his flesh and blood. He's a coward who the King of Ulster uses to keep some control."

"Who is the King?"

"O'Donnell. I've never met him, but his reputation

is…"

"I've heard of him," Dulca interrupted. "We'll be ready for battle."

"What warriors there are will protect what the chieftains have taken from their people."

Dulca frowned, waiting for her to continue.

"This is not like a Norse settlement where guests and families are welcome to feast in the longhouse. My father does not even mix with his children. He barely knows me."

"Easier to kill him then," Dulca said.

"Suppose," Sonas whispered. *Could she, though? She was here to use a blade to draw blood and take a life, would she be able to? Dulca expected her to be vicious. He brought her to complete her vow for revenge. Could she go back on her word? Would she murder her father? What would Ultan think? Would he hear she was in her homeland?*

"Stay by the ships," Dulca ordered Sonas, while others readied themselves for a march further inland. "I'll send for you when all is safe."

As soon as they rounded the headland, people would be frantic: scuttling into hiding, pulling valuables, children, and pretty girls into hideaways. Her father by his fireside for a parley or discussion on what new things the Vikings wanted. He'd refer to her sale and Ultan's promise that other Vikings would not raid them again.

Pah! More of Ultan's lies. He had no authority to offer such things. She should hate him for his lies. Should loathe the coward…but she couldn't. Try as she might, Sonas missed his hard body against hers, missed the sweet tender kisses, and his lingering thrust between her quivering thighs. There was a loneliness like never before. She had more power than she thought possible, and yet…she was destitute without the one she loved.

Sonas reached for Dulca as he passed. His eyes were kind when she smiled upward. "What are you thinking?" she asked, suddenly cold and fearful.

"I'm thinking nothing at all," he said. "I'm ready for whatever lies ahead. The gods have led me here. Why? What's in the pretty head of yours?"

"Come," she suggested and took him to one side where others might not hear them well. Tears filled her eyes as she sighed and came to terms with her troubled soul. "Let me go with you. I might save bloodshed."

"No," Dulca replied and touched her cheek. "You're too precious to me. Please do as I ask, and trust I'll keep my word as best I can. I'm not like Ultan the Fearless. I will keep my promise. You think I'm a beast, but I'm also a good leader of men. There is no sense in losing warriors in unnecessary trouble. From what I know…and what you told me, we will only visit and barter or trade. What you choose to do when you see your father is up to you."

"Thank you," Sonas whispered. "For bringing me home, for listening, for understanding…thank you."

Dulca leaned down and kissed her forehead. "I've always asked you to tell me the truth," he said. "I hope you'll not send me into a trap?"

Sonas gasped. "Never."

"Good." He chugged his thick leather chest armor to a more comfortable position. "Once I send for you, there must be no worry on your beautiful face. You must stride into your father's dwelling with the confidence of a queen. You hear me? No wrinkled forehead or teary eyes. You are a Norse. Wife to a jarl. Ruler of Upvhal.

Be strong."

Dulca fixed her sword tighter on her back, hugged her tightly, and asked, "And when you see me again, you will shout out as loud as you can whatever I tell you. Yes?"

"What?" she asked.

"In your language, you will say the words I shall give you. You must shout out for all to hear. You promise you will...for me?"

She nodded. "I promise."

Dulca kissed her while the surrounding men whooped battle cries into the sunlight.

Chapter Twenty-Four

Leave things be

"There's been no word of Dulca?" Ultan asked a drunk Helga. "You've hardly sobered these past few weeks. Everyone is concerned." He did not mention the mushrooms and potions she'd gotten from the healer made her dance naked in the forests.

"No news of Sonas either," Helga moaned and filled her horn cup again. "You've been judging the Upvhal disputes. Good. Arden would like to see you making important decisions."

"Helga, we need to talk," Ultan said, sitting in his father's seat by the fire pit.

"No," she said, facing away. "There's no need. Let's just leave things as they are."

"Your people are worried."

"They're no longer mine." She sniffed and wiped a dirty hand across her face. "No one cares about me."

"If you continue with foolishness—" Ultan started, but he couldn't finish his sentence. "What can I do to help?"

"Go after her," Helga said. "Bring her back."

"You mean Sonas?" he asked because of her slurred words. "You want me to find her?"

"Who else? He took her. You abandoned the poor creature, but he took her from where she belonged. Here with me. And I want her back."

"She'll come with Dulca when he returns. She's gone to kill her father."

"Huh!" Helga slumped so far down the chair she slinked onto the rushes. She lay on her back and cried. "He knows," she sobbed. "The worst punishment was stealing Sonas. He knew taking her would hurt me more than taking Upvhal. He's clever. A truly ugly beast. She saw. He left me here in Niflheim without her. Living. But not wanting to."

Ultan kneeled, hoping she would rise off the floor, but he knew even if he suggested, she would not move. "Helga. You're making a hell for yourself. Niflheim is not a place unless you linger there. I love Sonas, too. You must stop and rule Upvhal well. If Dulca returns, he will take Upvhal. Mother, please?"

"You say you love her," Helga half laughed and half cried. "Yet you left her to be swallowed up by the Beast. She had no choice but to be his woman."

Those words stabbed Ultan's heart. He held his chest as if shot with an arrow.

"She sailed with Dulca for me. I could keep my precious power seat. She left to take his mind elsewhere and to protect me," Helga said, allowing tears to flood her cheeks. "Sonas cared when she knew I needed her. She never once hurt me. Never once treated me as second best...to you."

"To me?" Ultan asked.

Helga sat and leaned against the nearest bench and held her dripping nose. She answered in a slow voice, cracking under the heavy words. "She loves you and only you."

Ultan leaped to his feet. *Despite everything, Sonas*

loved him. Helga may be drunk and upset, but she knew Sonas' heart…didn't she?

"Are you sure?" he asked. "She loves me? Still?"

Helga nodded, and her filthy blonde hair flopped forward. "She was in my bed, but she wanted to be in yours. I never asked her because she would not lie to me. When you left, she was a broken woman. Sonas cursed you, but she watched the door, the path, and the harbor for your return. She listened for your name in conversations and even asked for the healer to be sent. The only reason she agreed to be Dulca's woman was for me—it was not out of hate for you. I've wanted you to think it was out of spite or bitterness, but no. As much as I'm hurting…Sonas loves you and always will."

Ultan sat with his head in his hands. *By the gods, his heart was sore. What could he do or say? Sonas was not here, and he could not win her back. Jarl Dulca was too powerful and, much as he felt better, Dulca would beat him in any warrior contest for Sonas. He missed his red-haired Celt with every breath and longed to see her smile every minute of every day. Yes, he had fucked the shield maiden with Finnegan, but it was a release, a man's way of forgetting. If Sonas would have him, he'd go to her, no matter where she was…*

"She cares for you, but here you are sitting alone…" Helga said. "You wonder why I cry all the time. If I were you, I'd never have let her go. I wouldn't be sitting here waiting. I would travel across the widest ocean…I'd give up all I am for her and would demand Dulca give her back…if she loved me…But she does not want me!" Helga thumped the ground and flung her cup into the fire.

"I'm afraid," Ultan said. "I've lost everything,

sacrificed all, and there's nothing I can do…"

"You must win her back," Helga said, spittle resting on her chin. "You've done nothing to deserve her."

"And she'll have me?"

"I thought I could survive if Upvhal was mine. I was sure I would cope if I had power. But I cannot breathe," Helga heaved out more sobs as Ultan stood helpless. "Sonas sacrificed herself for us both. She gave herself to me…to save you, and offered herself to Dulca. I'm grateful, and this is the only reason I'm telling you. One of us needs to love her the way she needs, and I cannot. You must love her."

"How did she save me?" Ultan murmured.

"I could never harm the person she loves the most," Helga said, the fire dancing in her eyes.

"After Arden…I was next?" Ultan's right hand searched for his sword, but a cold iron blade slid against his cheek.

"Don't move," the shield maiden's voice said.

Where had she come from? The voice was familiar and was his favorite shield maiden. She guarded her mistress well. However, there would be no way she'd hurt him.

"Get up," she said. Helga remained in the rushes on the floor. "She's drunk and has no idea what she's saying. Leave her be."

Ultan flung the blade away from his throat. *Women were his torture. Sent by the gods to ruin everything.*

"Go get your precious Sonas," the shield maiden said. "Leave or I'll kill you myself."

Ultan stood tall. "Do not threaten me." He turned and spat into the fire pit. "Upvhal needs me here. Helga can't be left alone like this." He swept his hand toward the woman he considered a mother. "If I go, I'll not be forced by the likes of you."

Helga moaned in her drunken slumber.

The shield maiden reluctantly nodded, then gazed into the flickering flames. "I'm content because I know Sonas will be the death of your soul one way or another."

Chapter Twenty-Five

Sonas of the Flames

The earth was damp after the rain, and the sunlight dappled through the full oak trees. The clearing was familiar. She played in the long grasses as a child and ran wild with some of the village children. Her childhood was carefree; she made forts in the hay, rode horses bareback, and swam in the sea. When other children worked, Sonas learned needlecraft and drawing.

As a child, she held much more power over her destiny than she did when her cycle of blood came. Everything changed when she became a woman. She was waiting again. Powerless. She was home and yet she wasn't.

She paced over and back while some of the party lay in the shade and snoozed. The sword was heavy in its sheath at her back, and the small axe hanging from her belt clashed off her knee with each stride.

"The air smells fresh," someone said.

Sonas sniffed the breeze. "Fresh, salty, and full of promise."

Darkness fell, and Sonas reluctantly joined the storytelling beside the campfire. A noise in the undergrowth alerted the guards, but the worry was short lived. The messenger from Dulca returned. "You are to come with me," the man said. "The rest of you are to mind the ships. There might be trouble."

The messenger stole a horse, and Sonas and he rode into the night. Sonas' throat constricted in sadness as they trotted through the village. Compared to Upvhal, her people lived in hovels. Dirt or stone huts looked unpleasant in the smoky darkness. Her father had long since been burned out of the castle. The wooden fort was not much more than a few barricades made of mossy posts and stakes in the ground. A severed head sat on top of one pole, and the stench followed them as they passed by. The victim was unrecognizable to Sonas because of the decay and foraged flesh.

Dulca's booming voice and his giant stature was hard to miss, even in the dark. Fires blazed and groups of Celts and Vikings mixed around them. There was a smell of cooked meat, and unwashed hordes mingled with the smoke.

"Here she is. Queen Sonas, my Flame-Haired-Maiden," Dulca shouted.

Every eye was upon her as she slid from the horse.

"Come," he said, beckoning for Sonas to stand next to him. "Do you remember Sonas?" he called to the gathering crowds.

Sonas did not recognize a single face. Her mind raced as she searched for her kin and companions. Someone called, "Yes. She is Sonas O'Neill."

Dulca nuzzled his nose against her neck, and she shivered more. "Tell them you are now a queen. Shout out loud. You are my representative here. You will rule as my queen. Tell them."

"What about my father? And the Lord O'Donnell?" she asked and squinted into the groups of people for those who might not like such statements. "I cannot rule here. What about Upvhal?"

"Do as I command," Dulca said and gripped her arm. "Tell them you're home. Wife to a jarl. A king of sorts and they will be ruled by you, their blood, but also a wife and queen. Say it now."

"Helga?" Sonas whispered.

"She's my wife in Upvhal. You're my wife here. Astrid…"

A man moved forward into the firelight. "Sonas," he said. "Welcome home."

"Cousin Oisin," Sonas said. She was delighted to see a friendly ally. "Where's my father?"

The kind expression changed to worry, and he pointed toward the entrance to the fort. "O'Donnell left his head, but took the rest of him for his hounds."

Dulca nudged Sonas forward slightly and ignored her cousin and the news. "Tell them what I asked you to say."

"I am Sonas O'Neill. Sold into slavery, to a Norse called Ultan the Fearless. I was to be his sacrifice. However, all the many gods have answered my prayers. I stand before you as wife to Jarl Dulca. I call him The Beast and I'm home to rule the peninsula in Tyrconnell as his queen. I am Sonas of the Flames, and I'll avenge the murder of my father, and take your power back from the shit, Lord O'Donnell."

"I'm impressed," Dulca whispered. "Unsheathe your fine sword. Demand all fighting men come to your aid in seizing back whatever this muck heap is called."

Sonas did as he said. Her arm trembled as she shook her sword. "I ask for you all to send word far and wide— the Norse settlers of Bun an Phobail will cease to bow to the tyranny of the chieftains who do not care for their people. No Celtic man, woman, or child shall be sold to any raider or chieftain if they swear allegiance to me."

Dulca's mouth met hers in a passionate kiss, like he might eat her face. He then lifted her high up on his shoulders and paraded her around whooping battle cries and Norse blessings. Sonas was weak and slipped a little from her perch. The drink or the impassioned words she used made the people agree and they roared in unison with their Norse plunderers.

"There'll be a gathering and feasting here for the next seven days. Bring all your sons, fathers, cousins, and fighting men to these fires and the fort. There's work to be done and land to be reclaimed!" Dulca shouted into the night. "Sonas of the Flames is home and shall be your true and beloved queen."

Dulca carried Sonas through the welcoming people to a tent in the farthest corner of the settlement. He put her down like a sack of corn and removed his armor. He grunted, cursed and talked about the jobs to be completed. Sonas could hardly breathe, the world spun out of control. *Nothing made sense.*

"I am like the slave girl who was carried into Upvhal," Sonas muttered when Dulca nudged her to speak to him. "Do you know what you have done?" she asked, letting go of the sword. The metal clunked at her tired feet. "You think I want power? Don't you realize the armies of O'Donnell will come for me?"

"I don't care," Dulca said with a sneer. "You'll thank me, and I hope O'Donnell wants a battle." He roared into Sonas' face, "We fight! Valhalla awaits!" He was all fired up by his speeches. "Strip. I'm ready to fuck."

Sonas slid off the sack of corn and bent to pick up

her blade. "No," she said. "Get out."

Dulca's bare chest heaved with his quickened breathing. "What?"

"I am Sonas of the Flames, the Queen of Tyrconnell and I command you to leave."

With a dumbstruck expression Dulca stormed for the tent flap, muttering under his held breath. "Women."

Just as Sonas relaxed her battle-stance and lowered her weapon he turned and roared like a berserker. In a tantrum he stamped like a stubborn child and thumped his chest in a fit of rage.

Sonas chuckled but hadn't the strength to lift the sword. "Just leave," she commanded in a determined tone. "I rule here now and have my say over who I fuck and when. Out. Get."

"But…but you're my woman!" Dulca's eyes bulged and the veins in his thick neck looked strained. "I gave you all of this. You owe me." His arms flailed over his head, and he screamed again.

Sonas smiled and sighed. "When did I agree to your terms? What deal did we strike? Is Sonas of the Flames still a slave or is she a queen?"

Dulca paced the earthen floor his temper still evident in his reddened face.

"Am I a queen or not?" Sonas asked calmly. "Am I your queen?"

Dulca's gaze was reluctant but after a few tense seconds he nodded.

"Then you know what your queen commanded you to do." Sonas turned her back and did not move. "Out."

Without delay there was the sound of flapping tent leather and when Sonas peered around, Dulca the Beast was gone.

Chapter Twenty-Six

The First Wife of Three

"I'll wait forever, Sonas," Ultan whimpered to the starry night. "You are my greatest love, and my hardest sacrifice, you must know I'll always love you. Forever."

Nightly Ultan stood on the battlements and spoke to the memory of Sonas and begged the gods for her to be part of his destiny. He imagined her sweet lips under his own, those long legs circled his waist, the smell of her hair, the beat of her breast against his.

"Someday, my happiness," he promised the night. "Sometime soon, we'll be together, and I'll never be afraid again."

Earlier in the day, impulsive Helga decided to take her young sons to visit Uppsala. "Before one of my maidens murders you in your bed," she joked. There had been no ceremony, no fuss. *Ultan was now the ruler of Upvhal. This was what he'd wanted, wasn't it? Yet, something was missing. A hole lay between him and true contentedness.*

Bjorn joined him in the twilight, but he was restless. As a young warrior, he wanted battles and to travel across the ocean. "I'm praying for Dulca's return, too," he admitted to his father from the shadows. "I'll raid with him when he does."

Ultan nodded and slapped his son's back. In silence,

they watched the waves and calm tide coming in.

"But first, I'll go to Fiordland and see to the amber?" Bjorn asked.

Ultan had not considered his hoard or how he might reach Valhalla in a long time. His sons needed him. There was much to do before he would feast in the halls of his ancestors.

"We have a good plan," he said to Bjorn.

"Loki will either claim Fiordland or come here to Upvhal," Bjorn said. "He's been quiet. Plotting something. I will take some of the best warriors with me, as he has not gone far."

"Yes, Loki will be a problem," Ultan said with a yawn. "But he'll come here. He does not know about the amber, and Fiordland is useless to him. Upvhal is what he wants. I would say you should remain here. We need all swords in Upvhal. Also, Dulca might return soon, and you would be here to raid."

He didn't want Bjorn to venture far. He'd do all he could to keep him close and safe.

Bjorn scuffed his boots on the dried earth. "I'm not a miner, a farmer, or a fisherman. I want to fight," he said with a pout. "With the handmaidens gone, there's no woman of status here for me."

"There are many pretty girls," Ultan said.

"Humph!"

"We both must be patient."

"A ship?" Bjorn asked and pointed out to the open ocean. Suddenly the warning horn sounded. "Friend or foe?" Bjorn asked and took off at a run for the dock.

Ultan returned to the longhouse. *Whoever owned the ship was Norse, and he would need to receive the visitors and their tribute to Upvhal. But Dulca would not return in one lone ship? He would hardly limp home alone. It might be Sonas. She may have been sent homeward and Dulca sailed on to Alba or England.*

The servants stoked the fire and placed bread and milk on the long table. He asked for his special silver goblet, put his prized fur over his shoulders, and fidgeted with the large gold ring on his thumb. *Who was coming? At night? What could they want? Their guards and warriors could cope with one shipload of fighting men. But perhaps more ships were lying in wait? No more horns sounded. One ship, one crew…but who? If Sonas was aboard, he'd sing Odin's praise forever more.*

An excited Bjorn strode into the great hall. In his wake were a handful of warriors and shields. When they stood apart, a young, attractive woman bowed her crowned head.

"This fine woman is Astrid. Wife of Jarl Dulca," Bjorn said and beamed from ear to ear at the beauty. Ultan could see his attraction, but she did nothing for his loyal cock. Astrid was also young enough to be his daughter. Dulca was indeed a beast. The pretty thing was little more than a child.

"Welcome," Ultan said, gesturing to Helga's vacant seat. "Dulca is not here. I am Ultan the Fearless. And you have met my son, Bjorn."

Her smile was friendly, but her eyes were sharp.

"Thank you. I brought no tributes, for I am in my husband's realm. And I know who you are," she said. "Please excuse me for coming in the dark, but I had no choice." She shook off her fine cloak and sat with elegance. Her scent was strong and like a foreign spice. "I'm exhausted," she continued. "I'll ask you for some nice food and a good bed?"

From the way she spoke she did not expect it to be a simple request.

"She can have mine," Bjorn offered with a grin. "You're safe here, Astrid. Father is ruling until your husband returns. We were watching for him and saw your ship."

Her expression was patronizing when she said, "Isn't he a sweet boy?"

Ultan could not help smirking at his son. *Poor Bjorn. What arrogance this young woman had. Dulca liked feisty wives.*

"Can we do anything else for you?" Ultan asked. "These people can sleep here in the hall."

She shrugged as if she did not care where her entourage would find shelter.

"What else do you need?" Ultan asked.

"I wish to eat, sleep, and wait on my jarl."

"Bjorn, show this maiden to your chamber and bed," Ultan said mischievously. "Servants will bring you some provisions. Rest well."

"We'll return to the ship," a warrior said, and they all turned on their heel to leave.

Astrid did not acknowledge them and followed a downtrodden-looking Bjorn.

Ultan commanded the servants to go to bed. Alone again, he watched the flames and imagined Sonas' flowing hair, and sipped his honeyed milk. *Why was Astrid here?* Something happened for her to flee Dulca's first stronghold. Something sinister and her husband would return soon. Sonas would be back then, too. From what Ultan saw of Astrid, there would be sparks between the two women. Without question, Dulca's young wife would not accept Sonas. Then, Jarl Dulca would be in trouble. Ultan could offer to reclaim his prize. He would help his jarl yet again and take back his love, his sacrifice, his greatest love. Yes, Astrid might support Ultan in the quest. He would drink to the future. The gods were finally listening to his plea. All would be well soon enough...

Chapter Twenty-Seven

Good and True

Avoiding a man as big as Dulca was difficult in a small settlement. Even with the hordes of warriors coming over the last three days, his bulk was visible whenever Sonas took sanctuary. Her cousin, Oisin, removed her father's head from the spike and buried the skull somewhere decent. With nothing to busy her time or hands, Sonas' mind spiraled in despair. She managed to get a better tent in the opposite corner of Dulca's. The taut hide leaked in the Tyrconnell rain falling most days, but when she closed the flap of greased skin, the world was shut out.

Oisin was her only kin left. "The rest fled or were driven away," he reported. "They may return, as they know you are here. Although many are afraid of the heathen savages."

"They weren't the ones to take my father's life," Sonas said. "Mind you, I did come back to kill the bastard, but I doubt I could have done…"

"And you are their leader…?" Oisin began. "He made you a queen?"

"Yes," Sonas said as she smoothed the wrinkles in the front of her dress, and she examined the mud on her boots. "How long do you think until O'Donnell attacks?"

"Who knows? The food and ale will run out soon.

The marauders have crawled out of the forests, and they're not going to be happy for long. You know the rivalry between the clans, and then there're the Norsemen...this pot is boiling. Does Dulca have a plan?"

"I should ask him," Sonas said.

"You've suffered a great deal," Oisin said.

"I know you see the bed, my sword, my brooch, my attire..." Sonas said, "and you think I'm doing well. And yes, the gods have cared for me, but times have been difficult, too. I've had to be strong and fight for my life."

"I've no doubt. Is the giant Dulca really your husband?"

Sonas nodded. "I hardly know him. He is the jarl of the region I was taken to. He claimed Helga and me as his second and third wives. Helga is the ruler in Upvhal and she is stepmother to Ultan the Fearless."

"And she remained in Upvhal?"

"I'm not sure how she will cope without me."

Oisin scoffed.

"I was her handmaiden. Helga depended on my counsel," Sonas snapped. "She only agreed to Dulca's proposal because I was part of the agreement. She loves me."

Oisin grunted.

"What am I to do?" Sonas asked the gods, as well as her cousin.

"Speak with Dulca. He keeps the men content. But they are on a knife's edge with talks of fighting and battles. They've stolen anything of value and are looking to load what little grain and supplies we've left into their longships. You need to speak to him. Many people will rely on those winter stores. We'll starve."

"He took me home. He promised not to raid..."

Sonas lifted the opening to her tent and sanctuary. "I should have known better."

"They're not pillaging. Not murdering. They're just taking," Oisin added. "Please don't tell him I've asked anything of him, or you. He may get angry."

"Coward," she muttered under her breath, and she marched across the muddied clearing to Dulca's side of the settlement. "Dulca?" she roared. The one time she wanted to talk she could not see him. She cursed and kicked a wooden bucket out of her way. Gruff startled and growled.

"Sonas," a voice said to her left. Gruff hunkered down, the hair on his back and neck raised in anger, his bark sharp and menacing.

"Loki," Sonas replied with a nod to his companions. "Is Ultan with you?" she asked as her tummy flipped in anticipation.

"He was dying in Fiordland when we saw him last," Loki said, sucking his rotting teeth and moving too close.

Gruff snapped in warning and Loki raised his foot. Quick as a flash, Sonas stood between them and shouted, "No!"

Closer to Loki, she smelled death from his clothes, and he leered. Sonas reached for her sword and gripped the hilt. "Stand back," she ordered. When he did, she asked, "Why are you here?"

"We answered Dulca's call," one of Loki's men said. "Arrived on the morning tide. We knew where to come."

Sonas held her nerve while sweat dripped down her back.

"Dulca tells us he's ready to defend this place," Loki said, his inked face scrunched in disbelief. "He wishes to build a rich settlement. He'll be looking for a good man to rule here for him."

"And you wish to be the man?" Sonas replied unsheathing her sword. The warriors smiled and nudged each other. Gruff growled continuously, and the air was thick with tension. "I'm home and I rule here," Sonas said and brought the tip of her blade right to Loki's chin. "Perhaps you've not heard. I'm Dulca's wife. I'm your jarl."

Loki's gasp thrilled Sonas. "And Helga is his wife in Upvhal," she added.

"He's depending on women?" a warrior asked.

Dulca's shadow cast over them all before Sonas could reply. He placed a hand on Sonas' shoulder, encouraging her to lower her weapon. "I see you've met old friends," he said to them all.

Loki paled. Gruff stopped growling. Sonas held Dulca's arm and said, "That weasel is no ally of mine."

"Then slit his throat," Dulca said.

Loki buckled at his knees and leaned on his companion for a brief moment. "Please?" he begged quickly. "I came to pledge allegiance to you, Jarl Dulca."

"Ah, you're here to fight my enemies then, not my wife?" Dulca said with a laugh and pointed towards his camp. "Good. Let's eat."

Sonas held back. Gruff and Dulca stayed beside her like protecting beasts.

"I was looking to speak with you," Sonas said in a shaky voice.

Dulca lifted her into his arms, her feet dangled, and Gruff lay down in the mud. Dulca hugged her and spoke into her hair, "You're the bravest and most stubborn woman I've ever seen. But you've got to trust me. I know you're cross, but you need to calm down."

"Huh! Trust you? Says the man who promised me there would be no looting."

"The men need to eat."

"You were irresponsible when you called these hungry men to a place with little supplies. And they filled your longships with our winter stores."

"Who is taking the stores?"

"I dunno. The camp's food will also run out. Am I to rule here or not? You must teach me how. Like sword skills, I have to know how to deal with scum like Loki."

"You were doing well. But next time, just slash any man who disrespects you."

"Put me down," Sonas complained, wriggling. "If disrespect is the reason then I'd have maimed you many times over."

Dulca laughed, and Sonas joined him.

"Loki is one of Ultan the Fearless' men," Dulca said.

"Yes, and they abandoned him in Fiordland when he was dying," Sonas replied, sadness seeping into her soul. "There's no loyalty in men like Loki."

"Didn't Ultan leave you in Upvhal?" Dulca said, holding Sonas' cheek in his palm. "My beautiful red-haired Celt, your first lesson in leadership is…select those close to you with wisdom. Pick only those who will respect and stay true to you, those who will help raise you and keep you there."

"Is this why you brought me here?" Sonas asked.

"I tell you this to make you forget Ultan the Fearless and choose me for yourself."

Chapter Twenty-Eight

Choosing Love should be easy

"Bjorn has grown bigger since he came to Upvhal," Old Finnegan said as they watched the contests in the square outside the longhouse. "He fights well and likes to impress Astrid."

"He does," Ultan said as his forehead scar throbbed. "He must not value his balls. Dulca will remove them if there's a whiff of any trouble. And headstrong Bjorn will not listen to me."

"The boy is just a pup. He's not a threat to the likes of Dulca. You're a different story. Not only did you ignore going to raid with him, but you also sit in the power seat he left to Helga, and you want his new wife · as well."

"I've been thinking of little else. Loki is giving me sleepless nights, too. He trained Celtic captives as warriors…Do you think they'll be a danger to us here in Upvhal?"

"I couldn't say for sure," Finnegan replied as he played with the beads in his beard. "Depends on the men. But we Celts are canny. Cunning as foxes. They might use Loki for their ends."

"I'm praying they will," Ultan replied, and then he yelled for Bjorn to hold his spear higher. "Helga left rather than clash with me. Our shield maiden told me she'd kill me, but Helga took them all to Uppsala. Was she worried about me killing my half brothers? They are children."

"She's heartbroken," Finnegan replied. "Power was not all she thought it would be. Like all who crave leadership, once it happens, it is not enough. We all miss Sonas. The trip will do Helga good. She may return with new motivation."

"Helga said I should go bring Sonas back, said I should take her from Dulca," Ultan said, stopping to shout again at the contest rather than meeting his friend's eyes. "Could I? I'm worried. Sonas has brought such bad luck into my life. She's turned me into a coward. Yet I miss her. I've been a fool."

"Loki will not take Upvhal. He'll be petrified of an angry Dulca."

"Are you telling me not to annoy the jarl?"

Finnegan smiled.

"I won't go to Eire," Ultan said. "Sonas would not have me. I've hurt her. Dulca is the better man. Helga said she deserves someone to love her properly, and she is right. Dulca took Sonas home, to fulfill her vow. Helga told me he made her a wife, a ruler of Upvhal, and respected her enough to escort her home. He's given her everything I could not…or did not."

"He hardly knows her. He heard the rumors and knew we all cared about the wench. There were many reasons for him joining with her, but I doubt love is part of his plan. He's no fool and is good at keeping his reputation but I doubt he's capable of true love. I've been listening to Astrid speak with the other women."

"Oh?" Ultan said. "What did they say?"

"Talk with Astrid," Finnegan said. "I know you

think her a dangerous child bride, but she's older and wiser than she looks. Like Bjorn, she sees more than you give her credit for."

"I value your counsel, my friend," Ultan said.

"I don't like when people run from love and happiness," Finnegan replied. "Those things are more precious than gold, than power, than death. I think you made a big mistake leaving in the blizzard. However, now is more important, and you're right to choose carefully. Take your time. No rash judgments. Think on what I've said, but I must get back to the forge."

Ultan held his arm. "I'm grateful."

"I ask you only one thing. If you go toward my homeland, I might join you," Finnegan said. "I wish to see my homeland one more time before I die."

Ultan gripped Finnegan's sleeve. "I would be honored to have you with me."

The warning horns sounded and broke the games and their conversation. Astrid gathered her long dress and light shawl and headed for the docks. Bjorn put on his outer tunic, found his sword, and raced after her. Some curious people followed, but many returned to their daily tasks. Ultan noticed how their lives were unaffected by the politics or the comings and goings in the bay.

These simple folk had to survive, and their situations never changed. Did they care who was in charge? As long as someone took the cloak of responsibility, did they even notice? If the gods appointed someone, they simply trusted they were the right choice. They had a much simpler life as a merchant, trader, or weaver. He would find a role for himself once Dulca returned. He would stand aside, as, like Helga, he saw there were more important things in life. Finnegan was right. Sonas and their love were worth fighting for. He'd fight Dulca or anyone for love. He'd demand her back. Sonas was his prize and his woman. Yes, he'd be ready for whoever came into the longhouse from the dock.

The warning horns boomed again and again, signaling a sizeable force of ships approaching. Ultan reached for his sword and large shield. *He should have put on armor, but there was no time. His stride to the shore gave him strength and as he breathed in the fresh Upvhal air, he promised to protect the place with his last breath.*

He needn't have worried as the banners flying were Dulca's. His fleet was back. Ultan's spirits shifted, and he was suddenly vulnerable. *Sonas would be aboard. What would she do when she saw him? Would she still curse him? Would Dulca accept his excuses? Would they both spare his life? He needed to find Bjorn and warn him to remain calm, whatever the outcome.*

Out of the corner of his eye, he spied Finnegan watching the sails come ashore, too. "Finnegan," Ultan called out. "Find Bjorn. No matter what happens, tell him to be wise."

"I hear you, Ultan the Fearless," his friend shouted.

He was telling Ultan to be brave. How did he know what to say? Whatever his fate, Ultan would stand tall and accept it. Seeing Sonas would be enough. Like Finnegan wanted to see his homeland one last time, if he saw Sonas one more time...He'd sacrifice himself for their love. Yes. Finally, he was certain about what he had to do.

Dulca stood on the prow of the largest ship. His hair flew free in the wind and his tall stature was visible from a respectful distance. He was alone, shouting instructions to the men.

No Sonas? Ultan was close to tears. What had Dulca done to his woman?

Dulca searched the shoreline with his gaze. Astrid called out and Dulca jumped from the boat (before the ropes were tied fast) and ran the length of the wooden platform. Astrid hurried to greet him, too. *Was it the excitement of lovers? No. Then what?*

Dulca scooped the young girl up into his arms. Her feet trailed the ground, and he mouthed something into her hair. Reluctantly, Ultan looked elsewhere to locate his Sonas. *Where was she? There were no females in the crews. None. Where was Sonas?*

Astrid and Dulca edged through the welcoming throngs, and Ultan stood forward to greet his jarl.

"Ultan," Dulca said with a wicked grin. "You've cared for my women in my absence. Good!"

"We did not expect you," Ultan said, smiling back. "Helga has gone to Uppsala for the priests to bless her new position."

Dulca did not look convinced, but he did not flinch or seem angry.

"I could not sail when you called. I was unwell in Fiordland, but I came as soon as I could." He sounded childlike, making excuses. People would hear his apologies and tease him later.

"And took over from Helga?" Dulca asked, his large forehead wrinkling in suspicion.

"I stand aside. My jarl is back," Ultan said with a bow. He hurt his heart when he lowered his head.

"You don't seem happy, Ultan the Fearless," Dulca said with a wink. "Come. Let's eat. I'm hungry."

139

Ultan stood his ground and looked toward the ships. "Sonas," he said with determination. "Where is she?"

"You wish to see my red-haired Celt." Dulca leaned onto Ultan's shoulder. "Did she not curse you and call you Ultan the Damned?"

Astrid kept walking, and Dulca did not notice such was his sense of fun at Ultan's uncertainty.

"Fuck you, Dulca. Tell me. Where is my Sonas?"

Dulca's large finger prodded into Ultan's chest on each word, "She. Is. My. Sonas. My happiness. My Sonas of the Flames. And Ultan the Damned, you'll. Never. See. Her. Again."

Chapter Twenty-Nine

Dark, Bitter Waters

Sonas folded her arms and observed the progress. There was a full moon's cycle since Dulca had sailed with most of his power and wealth, leaving decrees, instructions, and Sonas in charge. *And alone.*

"The stone battlements are up," Oisin said. "Dulca will be pleased. He'll not recognize the place when he returns."

"I'm proud of all we've achieved," Sonas replied. "And the rain has stayed away for most of the time. How is the forge?"

"Lacking a good blacksmith."

"We need more weapons. O'Donnell and his ilk won't be far away."

"Loki returning with Tyrconnell fighters is a stroke of good luck."

"Are they loyal men?" Sonas asked her cousin.

His eyebrows were high in questioning her suspicions. "Of course," came his reply.

Sonas gritted her teeth. "I hope so. We need them and they know it. The other Irish marauders are getting bored. Send them out to hunt for the winter larders again. Maybe put some scouts into the villages and see what the nearest chieftains are thinking about what's happening. They will be busy if they won't dig ditches or build stone walls."

"Loki worries me, too," Oisin said as he dragged his hair into a tie at the base of his neck. "He is lurking about, like he's lying in wait. But for what?"

"For us to do all the hard work and then he'll strike."

"Against his jarl's orders?"

"Dulca set sail for a long voyage. There will be many moons before he could take revenge against anything Loki might do."

"Perhaps Loki needs culling before anything happens."

"He causes bother. I agree with you."

"Aye," Oisin said, shaking out the truth from his shoulders. "He'd think nothing of slitting my throat. Or yours."

"He's Norse."

"I noticed he's not been in Bun an Phobail for a few days. I wonder where he goes. His ship is in the port. He's gone on foot or stolen a horse or two."

"Are Ultan's men with him?"

"Those other layabouts who follow him around are still here. He took just one warrior with him. The biggest fellow. Were they Ultan's men?"

"Yes," Sonas said with a slight shiver. *Memories of her capture and Ultan's handsome face threw her mind into disarray. They always did. She should loathe the Brute from when he took her ashore in Upvhal, but his kind eyes and his gentle touch soothed her, made her care for her captor. The Brute's lies and eyes were her downfall. And yet, she still felt the same. It was complete foolishness and nothing she did rubbed away his influence in her heart and mind.*

"Loki likes to remind you...Ultan may be dead,"

Oisin said. "Surely you don't care?"

Sonas' heart pounded, she wanted to scream, and gulped back tears. *She cared for nothing more than knowing Ultan was safe and well.* "I care. I wish I didn't, but I do. Ultan the Fearless is still alive. I know he is. No matter what Loki says, I just know he has not gone to Valhalla."

The days without Ultan came and went. Fortifying the stronghold was successful. Warriors and their families from near and far came to the new Norse settlement. Sonas paid to have a longhouse built with a second story for chambers above the noise and smell of the animals. Her artistry was on display everywhere as she'd taken to carving the wood herself, and some men even completed the tapestries. Women also came to lie within the daubed walls and months flew by. The snows quickly capped the far mountains, and the rain turned to sleet next to the new boats along the shore. They were not huge Norse vessels yet, for the builders were apprentices, and Dulca's fleet would return in the better weather.

Although Sonas was their leader, there was little responsibility. Once people felt respected, they earned their keep. Contests and duels sorted the infighting, and soon the men relaxed into a peaceful existence together. Celts mingled with Vikings, and clans buried old rivalries into the foundations of a new thriving community.

The men Loki left behind silently assimilated back into the life of the fort. They trained newcomers in shield and sword skills. One was an expert with a spear, and another with a bow and arrow. No one mentioned the lack of Loki, Dulca, or any other Norse jarl at their fire pit.

Yet Sonas still searched the horizon every day. *Who was she waiting for? Dulca? Ultan? Helga? If she told the truth of her soul, Ultan was who she yearned for. The Brute was who she waited to see sail up to the new wooden pier. As much as she cursed and threatened his life, his safe return to these shores was what she prayed for. If he was by her side, in her bed, and with her, then her happiness was complete. Someday her prayers would be answered, and he would come. He'd rebuild their trust. He'd need her as much as she needed him. Someday... When these thoughts surfaced, she suppressed them. She chided herself. If Ultan did return, he'd steal her autonomy all over again. He would manipulate things to his advantage. She should be careful and calculating. As Dulca warned, she needed to be a cautious leader and surround herself with true and wise companions. Could rash and cowardly Ultan rise to the challenge? Could a man like him ever make her happy? If he was still alive, would he regret leaving her in Upvhal? Or he raided with Dulca and not considered her at all...Whatever way her heart faltered and fluttered, Ultan the Brute still brought her to the brink of hopeful and desperate tears.*

"The clans are quiet. This is a new port on their soil," Oisin warned for the fiftieth time, breaking her daydreams. "I know they fear revenge, but they could still attack before the snow."

"They still might," Sonas replied and combed her hair by the fire. "We need to place loyal and good lookouts on the shoreline and the paths to the villages. We must be ready."

"The hunts have gone well," Oisin said. "Another

reason for them to raid. We're taking their game."

"There's enough for all."

Oisin grunted.

"And Loki?" Sonas ventured to ask. "Any word?"

"None. His men are tight-lipped but don't seem to be plotting anything in his absence. I have spies, and they say all is calm. We're heading into the bitter weather in a good position."

"I'm extremely proud of all we've achieved." Sonas plaited the long strands of red hair and threw them over her right shoulder. "You and the people here have worked hard, yet something is stirring my blood. I can't settle my mind. Why have I the notion there is trouble lurking in the grey ocean out there? Mark my words, there is bitter darkness on the way…"

Chapter Thirty

Destiny

The messenger arriving at Upvhal was from Sonas' settlement. The man had lost an eye and all his companions. "Dulca's fort in Eire is under attack. Sonas of the Flames sends word to the jarl and his fleet for rescue or reinforcements. They are under siege."

"From whom?" Ultan asked, shaking the man's shoulders gently and then with more violence.

"Celts. Her people," the messenger whispered. "More powerful clans who don't want a Norse settlement on their soil. Dulca must come to their aid."

Ultan scoffed for Dulca had sailed off to raid many moons ago with the King of Daneland, and there was no news of him since. He had warned Ultan to govern Upvhal until Helga's or his return.

"Get this messenger to the healer," Ultan ordered while the servants readied the evening meal on the long benches for the warrior counsel. "We'll need to consult the seer, make sacrifices, and ask the gods for their guidance."

Despite his instructions, Ultan finally had a reason to go to Sonas.

"Find Bjorn," Ultan called from the top of the fire pit. "And Old Finnegan."

Ultan held his head in his hands and breathed

deeply. *His greatest challenge was upon him. Ultan the Fearless would rise again and he would fulfill his fate, with bravery and certainty. He could push his love for Sonas aside for a while until he deserved her in his arms. He was going to win his prize and the test from Odin.*

Astrid's small hand on his shoulder woke him from his thoughts. "You must go to Sonas," she said. "Dulca would wish it. I lost his home, and he cannot lose the base in Hibernia as well. Bjorn can rule Upvhal. Go kill Celts and rescue your greatest love."

Ultan took in her iron-colored eyes and perfect blonde hair and saw why his son was smitten. She was an ambitious vixen with the courage and cleverness of a wolf.

"Bjorn has told you too much," Ultan replied. "Sonas does not want or need me. She has called for her man Dulca."

"If you mean to make me jealous…I know they've never lain together. Dulca told me on their wedding night he was drunk and not capable of much. He wants her. He talked about how he would take her to his bed, but I know she was clever and kept just within reach but also resisted him. Dulca is not her *kærasta.*"

Ultan stifled a smile.

"Dulca is a man of truth and honor," Astrid said. "He's never lied to me, and he has asked the same respect from all his women. Helga could not love him and told him. Sonas said the same. She is yours, Ultan the Fearless, and always will be. The last she heard about you, you were dying in Fiordland. Why would she send for a weakened warrior who had abandoned her? Of course, she would call for her jarl, who has a fleet to come to her aid. But we all know you must go."

"And then Bjorn will allow you power here," Ultan said, sitting closer. "What would Dulca think of his treachery? He's my eldest son. I won't sail off, leaving him to the talons of a witch like you and the wrath of a powerful Beast like Dulca. He's a good son, and I won't let you destroy him."

"I told Dulca I care for Bjorn," Astrid said with confidence. "There's no danger."

Ultan stared. *Was she telling the truth? He wasn't sure.*

"You'll have to trust me," she said in her unnervingly wise manner. "And make your way quickly. The weather is on the turn. Bjorn is safe in my arms. You must go to Sonas."

Ultan wanted nothing more than to believe the beauty.

"Loki's uncle usurped the jarl from his home." Astrid went on, "And since Dulca left with the king to raid Alba, my spies tell me Loki's uncle funded his journey to Hibernia."

"What?" Ultan gasped. "Why didn't you tell me?"

"Sonas had enough resources to combat Loki's meager crew. There was no reason to burden you or send you out into dangerous seas until the season changed. Now I hear the Celts themselves have attacked Sonas. But if Loki and his uncle join them, she will need a larger force."

Ultan nodded and watched his best Upvhal warriors' grave expressions as they sat at the table one by one. "And we cannot leave Upvhal exposed, either. Perhaps this is their strategy? If we sail to Hibernia, we leave Upvhal vulnerable. Bjorn is too young to be here alone."

"He has me," Astrid replied. "And Helga may return

before the worst of the weather. She will bring her warriors and shield maidens. I don't know her, but the seer said she has found her strength from the gods in Uppsala. She'll ride back here, and we'll protect Upvhal with our last breath."

Courage pounded through his veins, and the scar on his forehead ached.

Bjorn's tall frame cast a shadow over them both. "Trust us, Father. Go," he said.

Ultan stood and raised a cup. "Men, we sail at sunrise. Make ready. We sail for our Jarl Dulca and to give aid to Sonas of the Flames. *Skål!*"

His cock was as hard as a rock with the thoughts of dangerous seas, the battles ahead, and holding Sonas again. He would touch her naked body, sense her writhing under him, panting and calling out his name.

"Wait for me, Sonas," he whispered to the fire pit. "I'm coming. Ultan the Fearless and the warriors of Upvhal will ride the waves and kill all of your enemies. I vow to never leave you in despair again. Wait for me, Sonas of the Flames. My powerful arms will protect you."

Chapter Thirty-One

Sailing to the Rescue

The settlement's stone walls held. Smoldering smoke rose from the unsuccessfully fired arrows to the thatch. A small rivulet of blood meandered toward the shoreline. Rain lashed into Sonas' face and her blistered hands reminded her of her voyage to Upvhal. She fought to survive and won again. Their enemy was gone (for now). Hope and ease replaced the smell of anger and fear.

O'Donnell's men did not have the heart to fight, and when the storm quenched the flames, Sonas stood on the battlements shouting against the grey skies. "I am Sonas, Norse bride to Jarl Dulca the Beast. I control fire, and I will burn all your homes with flames from my belly if I am not left to live in peace."

After a further day, the lookouts reported a quietness in the movements within the forests. With the pelting rain and howling winds, she couldn't ascertain if the siege was indeed over, but there were no more arrows.

"And they won't come from the bay as the seas are the roughest I've ever seen them," one of her warriors confirmed. "We can rest for a while."

They all wanted Sonas to close her eyes and sleep. *They had tried to get her to rest for days. Yet, she couldn't. On high alert, her limbs tingled, and her head was sore with responsibility.*

"I will not let Dulca down," she repeated over and over, and offered what little she had to the gods to grant her victory. "The men have fought well. Bring them more ale and meat."

"O'Donnell will raise more of the clans," someone whispered. "And the Vikings cannot return on those seas."

Just as Sonas drifted off into an uneasy sleep on the chair by the fire, the horns sounded, alerting them to the presence of many ships in the bay.

"A flag," someone roared. "From what we can tell, they are Norsemen."

Sonas' heart fluttered. *It was not Dulca, for the king had summoned him. Maybe the Norseman was Loki.* "Don't let them ashore!" Sonas roared as she reached for her sword. "Bring me a message horn."

The sound reverberated around the settlement and became one of communication. "Friend. Help," they said, and Sonas squinted into the slanting rain at the fluttering flag. "This must be Ultan the Fearless," she shouted. "I recognize his banner."

"Friend or foe?" someone hollered back.

"Neither," Sonas muttered as she held her head in her hands. *Loki could be setting a trap. He was most definitely behind the O'Donnell attack, for the men all fought like Norsemen. Loki was also foul enough to fly a false flag and take to treacherous seas. He was also a man of Ultan's. He sailed into the bay before for bad ends. What might have changed? If Ultan came was it to defend Dulca's new land, or not? If they delayed the fleet's safe passage, the ships might be washed further north and onto the jagged cliffs and rocks. If she let them ashore, her tired people would not need to fight in combat with fresh enough warriors. What would she do? What should she do?*

The call came again for instruction over the horns of reassurance. "Help. Ally."

"Let them ashore." Sonas relented. "There are too many of them to risk losing and too many to stop an attack. We'll have to trust their word."

Oisin stood scratching his red beard, dumbfounded. As the three Norse ships docked, Sonas searched the covered men on the prow of each vessel.

She would know the Brute from a distance…wouldn't she? There was his tall, lean figure in the first ship, standing with a long stick to steady him. Covered in furs and a large shield, she squinted to tell who the man was, and yet… her pulse quickened, and her fitte, between her legs, yearned like never before. Ultan had traveled the journey on similar seas before. He might have come to help her. He would also want her power seat. And could he want her, too? He'd left Upvhal and her bed so why come? Was he afraid of Dulca? Or did he want to take what was Dulca's when he had the chance? Whatever the reason, the first Vikings already strode ashore.

Against the biting winds, Sonas faced the first of their fleet with a stance and a look of iron. His covered head kept the elements at bay. The man sported a dark and long beard. As he took off his hood, a shock of dark hair fell forward. Large, calloused hands brushed his hair back and Sonas looked into the kind eyes she had longed to see again.

"Ultan the Fearless," she said as her voice broke with emotion.

"My Sonas." He bowed his head.

"Why?" was all she could say. Luckily, the torrential rain covered her face and the falling tears.

"Let's talk inside," Ultan said, pointing toward the dwellings. "I've come to help."

"I'll not let Loki within the walls..." Sonas said, and surveyed the warriors coming ashore and following their leader.

"Loki?" Ultan questioned. "Is he here?"

"He's not with you?"

"No."

"Then we can get out of the messy weather."

Sonas strode in time with Ultan's footsteps as she sheathed her sword at her back. She leaped over the ditch and scaled the footbridge like a goat. Ultan reached out a hand to help her climb the last stone battlement, but she ignored him. She jumped to the ground with ease and smiled to herself as he followed her into her longhouse. *How different it was being near him. With power, she did not fear or seek his approval. He came to help. Whether his reasons were selfish or not, Ultan was here. The greatest love she knew and would ever know. He risked his life on those seas and was...*

Ultan's hand enveloped hers. "Is all this yours?" he asked as she stood back and let the guards open the large inner doors. Ultan looked into the carved rafters of the longhouse. "It was not your father's."

"No," she said and shrugged off his grasp. Gruff came out of the shadows and wagged his tail as she took off her weapons, armor, and cloaks. Servants scuttled forward to help, and she asked for food and shelter for their guests. Ultan stood as she sat near the blazing fire pit. With purpose, she threw more logs on herself. "Sit,

Ultan," she urged, but Gruff sat at her heel instead.

Ultan eyed the dog with fear and rubbed his thigh. Gruff sensed an old foe and raised his hackles, but Sonas tutted, and Gruff stopped his angry greeting. "Sit," Sonas said again. "You are soaked. Take off those wet furs. Eat."

"Should we not be at battle while there is still daylight?" Ultan asked.

"Our enemy has retreated...for the present time," she replied. "Did Helga send you? Where is my husband?"

She picked those words with purpose, and watched his reaction. *Yes, he was jealous. Angry even. His gaze darted to Gruff and then his surroundings until his fingers curled into a fist at the mention of Dulca. Yet she waited for his answer. He was uncomfortable. Almost...afraid? Why was she happy? Did she enjoy seeing a warrior like him squirm? He deserved it. Didn't he? Yes, she enjoyed seeing him falter. She held the power.*

Ultan removed his furs and fixed his hair back into a leather tie at the base of his neck. *Sonas tried not to ogle his arms and the broad leather armor across his chest. Yet, she imagined him naked almost immediately, and her gaze wandered lower...He sat to remove his boots and shook the water from them onto the floor and did not answer. She could wait. Patience was one of her virtues.*

"As well you know, Dulca is with the king," Ultan finally replied. "Helga did not send me. I came because..." He leaned his elbows onto his knees. "I hold the power in Upvhal, but I came to your aid."

Sonas smiled as the fire sparked with the new logs.

"You sacrificed something you've always craved, Ultan the Fearless," she mumbled.

Ultan chuckled and wiped his hands on his trousers, and sat back as nervousness flickered across his face. "No. I came to reclaim my prize," he said. "Came for you, Sonas...because you're mine and I should never have lost you."

Chapter Thirty-Two

Forever Vow

Ultan's blood boiled when Old Finnegan embraced Sonas. She welcomed her old friend with open arms and a kiss on the cheek. Finnegan's gray beard glistened as he winked with triumph at Ultan.

"We need a blacksmith." Sonas beamed despite her tired voice. "The gods have answered all of my prayers." She stopped and stared. Ultan glared back, and then she said with glee, "…well, they answered almost all of my requests."

"What do you mean?" Ultan snapped. He should watch his words, for Sonas was fiery and had not taken well to his claiming her as his prize. She shouted and hissed and sent the hound into an almost full-blown attack again. Making her angry was dangerous, but he couldn't help himself. She drove him wild. "Answer me, woman," he said, spittle following the words from his mouth. "What do you mean?"

"Well…" Sonas said, her pretty face grimacing with false worry. "I prayed for your death on more than one occasion."

The men all hooted with laughter, and Finnegan slapped Ultan's back in glee.

She enjoyed tormenting him again with her clever tactics. He fell into them every time. She was a witch if ever there was one, a superb creature who made his cock soar, but one who he'd subdue soon enough. The battle had exhausted her, and she was beautifully vulnerable. He'd win her back...however long, he would work forever for his prize. She could play games and tease him, but her eyes told him she missed him as much as he missed her.

"And tell me, Ultan, did you ever get a woman to be your sacrifice?" Sonas asked. "Or did you just decide you didn't need to be a legendary warrior, after all?" His hold on her forearm was harsh, and she cried out when he pushed her back against the wall. Some of her men stood but did not come to her aid. Thankfully, he had banished the dog to the cowshed. He shouldn't hold her close...but he couldn't lose face in front of the men. Instead, he held her tighter and hissed into her ear. "Don't provoke me."

"Let go," she said, never faltering her gaze from his. Her resolve was firm, for she didn't wriggle or beg.

"No," he said, panting as the scent of her hair hit him.

Finnegan started a conversation about the weather to distract the group, but when Ultan looked at them, he sensed they wondered what was happening. *He wasn't sure about what the fight was for. His grip was supposed to be menacing, but it felt like a passionate plea to let him kiss her. He wanted to hold her in his arms like Finnegan had. He needed to have her lips on his.*

"Let. Me. Go," she said again. "You don't own me. I'm a free woman called Sonas of the Flames and a leader here in Tyrconnell. I'm no longer a handmaiden or sacrifice you can use. I'm not afraid of you, Ultan the Fearless."

"Pah! You can be brave when you're the whore to a jarl," he said and wrenched her even closer. The pace of her breath changed instantly. He had taken his teasing too far. He caused the pain blooming on her face. "I didn't mean…" he said. "I know you had no choice."

"I did. Dulca gave me options. He respects me," Sonas said.

His stomach clenched as her mouth lingered nearer to his chin.

"Dulca is a man of his word, a loyal man of courage, and I am honored to be his wife. I'm no one's whore."

"Yet you never let him hump you. Everyone knows," he whispered into the tight space between them. He wouldn't lower his chin to find her expression of shock, but her body tightened enough for him to sense the effect. "And stop fighting. Helga told me you care for only one man. Who might he be?" With both hands, he took her arms and placed them on his shoulders and held them there.

Sonas wriggled under his grasp, but he held her there until she relented. He chanced to rub his cheek against her hair and toward her ear. "Say you're mine, Sonas of the Flames." He sucked the little earlobe between his teeth and her whole body stiffened. He tenderly kissed the delicate skin his lips had found and muttered, "I was a fool to leave you. I'll never make that mistake again."

"Let. Me. Go," she said.

Ultan squeezed her hands and savored the smoothness of her skin against his palms but then released his hold. Instantly, she turned her back to him. *Did she wipe her face? What was she thinking? Why did she resist him when her body was his?*

She threw a cloak over her shoulders and left him openmouthed. He wanted to call after her and make her stop. *But ordering his Celtic princess was foolish. She had power, and it excited him beyond reason. At least he was in the same country, in the same place, and he could be patient. He had waited for her to come closer, and he could wait a little longer.*

A musician played a tune on a flute, and Finnegan nudged him back to the group. "Leave her be," he said. "She's exhausted and will need coaxing."

"Don't I know."

"She is loyal," Finnegan warned and handed him some bread.

"To Dulca?"

"Who else? He gave her a lot more than you did."

"Where's your mistress?" Ultan asked a servant girl. "Where did she go?"

"Every night she stands on the battlements," came the reply. "On the west with a view of the sea."

Ultan found his weapons and furs. *He would join her in the dark and make amends. The air would do them both good. He could be himself away from prying eyes and be kind. He would take her into his arms and promise to protect her, respect her, and love her. She'd give in. Just like when he'd seduced her in his childhood bed, she would become his woman. Again. And he would not be a fool. She would know his love.*

The sight of her standing on the stone wall with her arms outstretched toward the swirling ocean took his breath. Even in the moonlight, her flowing hair looked like flapping flames. *She was a queen of fire, his queen.*

As he walked closer, he silenced his approach and listened intently to her voice. She chanted. A loud bark stopped him in his tracks and took Sonas from her magic. *The fucking hound!*

" 'Tis me," he said. "Hold the dog. I came to speak with you. Alone."

"You hate to talk. You want action."

"I came to help you with the siege."

"You wish to know about battles. Although things are at peace, I don't know for how long. Don't worry, you may get to kill some Celts soon enough."

"There's only one Celt I seem to fight with," Ultan said and watched the dog growl. "And only one Celt I'm here for. Sonas, I'm bad with my words. I'm not like Dulca. I don't know the right way to treat a woman of status. I just know I...Can you stop your dog from menacing me? He almost killed me, you know. I'm supposed to be a fearless warrior, and between you and the dog, I'm a mess."

Sonas giggled. *She was happy in his presence. Progress.*

"Tell me something...Was I right about Helga?" he asked. "You know she murdered my father? You know, too, she wanted to take all from me? Was I not right to leave Upvhal? I couldn't have taken you in the snow. The weather was too dangerous. I almost died...I couldn't come back...Sonas, please?"

"You promised."

"And I'm here. To fulfill my vow to you. I'm here."

"What if you're too late? What if I don't forgive you? What if I let Gruff eat your innards?"

"And what if...what if...you let me stay here and love you?"

"Stay? You'd remain here for how long?" Sonas asked, turning to face him and making his cock harder than ever before. "What if I let you stay and love me? How long for? How long would you love me for this time?"

"For? Forever…" he stammered.

As she walked closer, his blood ran cold when he saw her troubled eyes and heard her ask, "Ultan the Fearless, you'd sacrifice everything and stay here with me forever? Are you making a sacred vow?"

Chapter Thirty-Three

Bed of Emotion

Sheer exhaustion took over when Ultan's arms surrounded her sobbing shoulders. "I'm not like you," she sniffed. "I'm trying to be strong, but I cannot be fearless."

He held her. She was finally safe and where she belonged...close to the Brute. She had missed his embrace. The loneliness since he left, came flooding back, all at once. The sadness choked her. Dulca would be angry, but the magic between her and Ultan had not been robbed by time or trouble.

She couldn't speak, which was a blessing. He was saying something, kissing her neck, and whispering promises. His frame was large, but she slotted in the crook of his chest, like a carpenter's best wooden joint. He rubbed her back. She clung to him, crying.

"Whist, my love," he sighed. "All is better. I'll never leave you again."

Sonas strained to listen as she sniveled back the emotion and wiped her face. The storms rose again, far out on the horizon. Large gusts of biting wind swept over them both, and Sonas buried her nose in Ultan's hair and neck. The scent she loved eased her, but the slanting rain drenched them both.

"Take me to your bed," Ultan said, held her cheek

and gazed into her eyes. "To sleep."

Sonas agreed and took his hand in hers. In silence, they ambled to her chamber, ignored the others, the brewing storm, and Gruff's growl.

Ultan loosened her brooch and took off the cloak. The ties at the back of her dress were tight and took time to come away. She sensed the cool air on her skin as a hand slipped the material from one shoulder, then another. She raised her arms, and he pulled the under slip up and over her weary head.

"Lie down," he said.

He placed tender kisses down her back, and she shivered. He wrapped her in the blankets and furs. Sonas was almost fully asleep as his warm weight slid in behind her on the mattress. A muscular arm covered her, and she heard him say, "I love you."

She awoke to find their positions had shifted, and his handsome nose was next to hers. The sight of him took her breath. *She loved him more than ever. How was it even possible? She needed all her resolve not to touch his stubbled jaw and kiss those full and parted lips. Thankfully, she could see neither his dark eyes nor chest, for the arch of his scarred eyebrow and forehead, the smell of his skin, and the presence of him were more than enough. She never wanted anyone more in all her life. Helga was pretty, Dulca was intriguing, but Ultan was...perfectly beautiful and...*

"You're awake," he said with a glorious smile. He touched the hair lying on her cheek and trickled the strand away. "I've missed waking up to find you beside me."

She smiled, and a tear ran past her nose.

His thumb wiped her cheek. "I hurt you."

She gulped letting her anger slip away, and she closed her eyes. His touch made the tremble worse. *If she could drift off again, she might have more strength to deal with him in the morning. Was his breath on her lips?*

His beard grazed her mouth. He kissed her with such care, Sonas reached for his face. Fingers slid across his ears, and his mouth fell to hers as her lips parted. She moaned as a passionate tongue tip slid in past her quivering lips. She wished he would sink deeper, but he disappeared. "Sleep," came the whisper with a peck on her shaking chin. "How I've missed you, my Sonas. Rest."

"I might change my mind," she lied. "I'm dreaming."

Sonas loved the morning light in her longhouse, but the chinks found the best view in all the world. Ultan's rippled muscular chest heaved in sleepy breathing. She lay watching him for a long while, recalling how many times she had ogled him in the past, and all the times she kissed down his body. *How she loved every inch of the marked skin. And, if she imagined any more of his thickness inside her, she would reach her peak without his touch. Together, their bodies were on fire. No matter what way he entered her—rough, smooth, awkwardly, quickly, or quietly, her body responded and needed more. Much more.*

The instinct to lie on top of him was too great. Her leg slid over his hip, and she rested her cheek against his heart. He touched her hair and tickled her spine and over her bare bottom.

Looking at him was a bad idea. His dark eyes were irresistible. His breath was warm on her cheek. He licked lightly across her lip, then stopped, panting. He waited. For what?

His hard cock was against the blanket, and she writhed and gasped into his open mouth. *She needed him.*

He still held either side of her face and glared with desire as she slid the scratchy blanket over his erection. She felt all his length until she gripped his balls. He groaned as she teased the tip of his cock between her folds. She was wet, and he felt good slipping the helmet of his cock over her pleasure. *He wanted her. She needed more. These feelings were sent from the gods and could never end. Her inner place throbbed, waiting on its guest. If she took her time, they would last longer. He was hard, thick, and more than ready. Could she stand the teasing? No. She could wait no more.*

She sat with care and clenched as she squatted slowly. She circled her hips and moaned as he entered, little by little. When fully sheathed, he bucked and moaned. He gripped her waist, and their joined movements were deliberate, languid, and steady. Every thrust was bliss, and he was deep and long. "I need more," he said and with noble purpose, he thundered her up and down on his full length over and over. She steadied her balance with a shaking hand on his rippling chest and rode him. She rubbed against his pelvis as he came hard, reached down and flicked a finger over her clit just a few times and unbearable desire rose and rose...until she tipped over the edge.

In one swift movement, he flung them both over until he lay alongside her. He took what little breath she had left. And when he kissed her with such passion; she wanted to die from happiness.

****

As the weak candlelight flickered shadows on the

walls, Ultan held Sonas. Listening to the strange sounds was the most important. Even in the sleepy silence, he heard noises; the slight breath of his woman, the creak of the wooden structure settling in to protect them, the crackle of a fire, the hoot of an owl. Two men were outside. There was a shuffle of shields and spears.

Two? No three? They were not Norsemen. The clunk of metal against wood...was different. He was in Hibernia, with Celts. With enemies. Yet he lay in the safest and most comfortable place in all the world. He took Sonas from all she knew, and she had slept on the floor with dogs. How terrible for her.

Ultan turned his face from the sleeping woman.

Even though she couldn't see him, he frowned and recalled the uncertainties she experienced. A lump formed in his throat. *When you care for someone, you experience their emotions too, or some of them. This was what shocked him in the beginning. A warrior did not like vulnerability. She was his weakness. He would explain all to Sonas in the light of day.*

He turned and rubbed a caring hand through her hair and shut out all his troubles.

The growl of the dog grew louder. Without fully wakening, Sonas sat up.

"What?" she hissed. "Gruff?"

Ultan reached for his sword from next to the bed. Its metal was cold and reassuring. His other held Sonas' shoulders. They both strained to listen. Gruff settled down again with a slight flop to the hardened earth floor.

"Most people are asleep, but there are men outside," Ultan whispered. "Two or three. Perhaps patrolling the settlement?"

Sonas nodded. Her disheveled hair sat at a funny

angle on the back of her head. Ultan smiled. "I can go and look…" he offered, but she took his hand in hers. "My job is to protect you," he whispered.

She did not mock his lazy bravery, but lay back against the feathered sack. The tip of a nipple visible, and Ultan put his sword down. He touched the circle of pink and as he traced a finger over the perfect nipple puckered. Sonas sighed.

"You are beautiful," he said. "And once I see you, all thoughts of battles and enemies are forgotten."

In the faint candlelight, small shadows flickered across her skin, and she was even more appealing.

"You know I was a fool," he said, "and Norse men rarely admit they are wrong."

She nodded. He braced himself, ready to leap from the furs. He saw her look at the scar. He held his thigh and said, "Yes, your hound's teeth made a gaping wound and it got worse when I was in Fiordland. The gods weakened me to the point of death, and I realized what was important to me; my sons, my legacy, but also…you. The most precious of all was you, my Sonas. I got wisdom in the end."

Still, Sonas remained silent.

Was she happy? Was she worried? He couldn't tell in the gloom what was going on. He didn't deserve her love. Yet he hoped she'd forgiven him when they humped. She forgot the past then. Yes, she did. How else could he show passion and love for her? A woman could not give herself fully unless she understood and loved the man she was with. Hadn't Freya complained she neither loved nor understood him? Sonas differed from Freya. She was nothing like any other woman. They were mating animals. But the lack of loving was a deep concern.

"Tell me what you're thinking," he whispered and swept a finger across her breast. She shivered. "Reassure me. You still want this old fool?"

"I cannot think," she said after an agonizing pause. "I see Dulca's anger when I do, and I always suffer because of your whims. I'm foolish."

"No," he said and lay next to her and kissed those soft lips.

"Dulca asked me to be wise," she said. "I don't think I'm listening to him. I can almost hear his rage across the ocean. He would be displeased that you're in my bed, but his anger would be worse because I'm not remembering his words. I told him I would always love you. He knows about us. But perhaps he was right…you are not the best man for me."

"This is the only truth. We're the best when we are together," Ultan urged. His heart thumped and his worry caught in his rib cage. "Do you care about Jarl Dulca?"

Ultan held his breath and waited for the reply. *Astrid showed some sort of loyalty to the ugly animal of a jarl. She did not fall into Bjorn's bed. What kind of hold did Dulca have over women? Helga said he had a large cock, but Sonas could not care about that…But why was she taking this long to answer him?*

"Do you love Dulca?" Ultan asked and sat up. "Answer me."

"No," she finally said. "But I care about his opinion."

"Finnegan told me he has given you more than I have. Wealth, status, power, and I have brought only pain. But I have always known you and I will achieve greatness together. Dulca sailed away, leaving you in danger. From now, we shall battle as one."

His knee coaxed her legs apart. "Let me show you how powerful we can be…"

"You just want between my thighs," she said with a hardened look. "I remember when you stole me. Back then, you had ambitions and dreams. You let nothing stand in your way. I never had those thoughts. Why would a Celtic woman have ambitions? I see I can have all you have and much more, and I shouldn't let a cock take power from me."

Ultan looked deep into Sonas's eyes and held her under him.

"I understand," he said as he sucked her warm breath into his mouth. He passionately sought forgiveness with his tongue. Sonas relented and surrendered to their rising desire. He broke free to reassure her again, "I heard what you said, and I will prove myself worthy of you."

As she kissed him, Ultan's mind wandered. *How in the name of all the gods would he ever do what he just promised? How could he ever give her reasons to love him fully again? How would he win his greatest woman back when he had nothing but his love to offer her?*

Chapter Thirty-Four

A Battle

Sonas could see her bare-chested warrior across the clashes and fighting men. The enemy had breached the stonewalls at dawn. There was little time to dress before Oisin burst in and screamed about the hordes climbing the battlements. Thing weren't as bad when they got outside. The frost was the biggest problem. Everything gleamed in a slippery, dangerous mess.

The coldness rose in smoke around the remaining fighters. Ultan looked fearless, as she saw him run a sword through a man's chest. The grunt and the slump of his conquest was thrilling. She could watch the battle because Gruff was busy at her heels. No man dared to raise his weapon against her. The screams she heard were not her own anymore because her warriors and Ultan's powerful arms were winning. She was silent and bolstered.

They were the victors. Again. The retreat was obvious, with a few stragglers stuck and flailing in defeat. Ultan's smile across the smoky gloom was like a dream. *How she loved him. She would be strong and not give in to his seduction, but their fate was inevitable. She would always be his woman, no matter what she said or how much she pretended to resist him.*

The broad bare chest was pink from the cold and

spattered with blood, and his eyes were no longer kind. They were wide and vicious. His dark beard was coated in muck and his braided hair flew free.

A raging man in battle was quite the sight. She thanked the gods he was on her side. Was the striding figure interested in who he was defending, or was he interested in a chance to battle for glory?

"Sonas," he roared. "Light the fires. We must feast. Celebrate our victory. We are done."

She was more interested in knowing who her foe was. Oisin scuttled about, bringing weapons from the forge to those who needed them on the defenses. She beckoned him over. "Who were they? No banner? Norse or Irish?"

Oisin shrugged but tried to look clever. "Does that matter? They've gone."

"For now," Sonas replied and inspected the docked ships. Two sustained damage before the alarm. Men lay injured in her path, but she strode on. The sheltered bay was awash with the incoming tide and the boats bobbed about. Gruff settled his barking and snarling, but his hair raised as she petted his head. "Good boy," she muttered.

"The storehouses were burned," Ultan said as he came to her side. "We're going to have a tough winter. The threat of attack and the starvation will be fun."

He didn't look bothered by the statement. His features were alive as he wiped blood from them with the back of his hand.

"You enjoyed the fighting," Sonas said.

"Battle is what we live for"—Ultan smirked—"war and a good woman."

Sonas couldn't help but touch his chest and sink into his arms. She held him tightly, thanking the gods silently for their survival. She saw a short cut on his collarbone.

"We must see to the injured," she said,

"And rest and gather our strength again," Ultan said, and his hand rubbed across the sword on her back and into her hair. "The hound protects you better than I could. Much as I wanted to see the animal dead, I think the hound has its uses."

"Any man who harms Gruff will suffer the consequences."

"Who taught you to wield a sword?" He stroked on and she melted despite the surrounding cold. "You can defend yourself well."

"Dulca," she muttered and broke their embrace. "If we have no supplies, and if we are not wanted in my homeland, is there any point in defending here? I have thought about Dulca. He had plenty of men to defend this place, but he left me only a few…"

"Warriors," Ultan said and touched her cheek the way she liked. "You're one of their blood now. But the Celts will accept you. In time."

Sonas shook her head.

"Dulca places his women in positions of power," Ultan said. "He's clever."

"Why?" Sonas snapped. "You think we're easier to manipulate."

"No. I mean, you're an extension of him. When his sons are not old enough to rule, he has wives. There is no man to remove."

Sonas nodded. *What was she to do? However long she was in charge would be too long. There was no hoard to hold a fighting band of men over the winter. Dulca had promised riches from the raids in Alba, but if the attacks were frequent, she would not have the means to pay the warriors enough danger money. They would not fight for glory under the leadership of a woman for long? Would they?*

"I've no hoard," she said in a low voice to Ultan. "I'm worried Dulca will not return in time to appease the men if these attacks continue. The Vikings might fight on, but the natives we have in the settlement will not be as eager to battle against their blood unless there is the promise of wealth or something to appease them."

"You are Sonas of the Flames," Ultan said and toyed with a strand of her hair. "Clever Dulca made you into a legend. Men will defend what they admire and fear. Make them do your bidding. You need to put on the face of strength you use against me and brazen it out. You might not wound a man with a weapon, but with those eyes, you can win many battles."

"Helga would say the same," Sonas sighed.

"She misses you, too," Ultan admitted and looked seaward. "I hope she has returned from Uppsala and is there to help Bjorn and Astrid."

"What?" Sonas asked.

As they walked back through the settlement, Ultan told her all the news.

"I'll have to defend this place for Dulca all the more. If he's losing his power elsewhere, he will be depending on me here."

Ultan scuffed his boots.

"Don't be jealous," Sonas said. "Come. We've too much to do."

"I'm not angry," Ultan replied. "I'm just thinking about what I want. I'm wondering what I can do or should do." He gripped Sonas against his freezing chest and kissed her full on the mouth.

She let her mind drift away from her problems.

When they stopped, he looked pleased with himself. "I know what my destiny is. You will make me a legendary warrior, Sonas," he said. "And together, we will make love and war."

Chapter Thirty-Five

Dealing with Power

The rough linen lined wooden bathing tub was ready, but she had lost the sliver of soap. However, she was clean, warm, and content when she stood from the water and took the drying cloth from the stool. Her clothes dripped on the line, washed by a servant, but the old tunic she heaved on was scratchy and did not fit well, but would have to do. *Sonas liked to be clean. Where was Ultan? Still feasting or arm wrestling, no doubt. She was too preoccupied to relax.*

She brushed and combed her hair through and wrung the long strands out again. Damp ringlets fell from her shoulders as she dried her tired feet. The captors murdered the injured prisoners who refused to speak. Ultan did the deed before Sonas ordered anything different.

"Dulca would do the same," he said when she protested. "They were O'Donnell's men. We spared one of the youngest to take him a message to parley."

Did she want to talk with the likes of O'Donnell, who was her father's murderer? He had saved her the trouble, but his viciousness was renowned. Did she have the strength to face the likes of him? She never wanted these responsibilities or struggles. A woman like her should marry and let her husband provide. The worst she would have to do would be to manage a few servants. And Ultan brought out the most unmanageable emotions. How could she be sure of herself when he kissed her? She disappeared into the love between them, like smoke or a puff of air. He might be bored with just one woman. Finnegan hinted at Ultan's wandering eye in Upvhal. Keeping him interested might not be easy. Had she the energy to try?

Steam still rose from the bathwater as she sat on the stool to plait her hair. Ultan's large booming voice reached her chamber before he did.

Was he singing? Drunk!

He stripped off his clothes and leaped into the bath with an enormous splash. Water cascaded over the top. As he sang, he lathered himself with the tiny remnant of found soap.

"Old Finnegan has no love for the O'Donnell clan. He fought at one time for a rival. His mood is much improved even though he has not found willing women for his bed," Ultan said. "I should wash my hair, too. There is blood, isn't there?" He continued to hum a tune, stopping to add, "You know Finnegan sometimes likes two *fittes* at once. He's a dark horse. Loves women."

Sonas sat back on the stool to listen.

"I should tell you I fucked a shield maiden with him an odd time," Ultan said, scrubbing his scalp. "These times were nothing like ours, but I needed…well…a distraction. And sure you bedded Helga and others, I'm sure you did."

"Yes," Sonas said, amused he was fishing for information as well as confessing. "And I took a husband," she said.

"Astrid said you'd not fucked with him. And Oisin

seems to think the same. They told me you were not with him in a bed," Ultan said, trying not to question or look at her.

Sonas smiled. "Did they?"

"Perhaps Dulca just told Astrid to keep her happy," Ultan said and rinsed his hair.

He was a fine man. Sonas couldn't help but marvel at his handsome square jaw and rippled torso. Dulca was his rival in every way. There was a pang of guilt, but then images of Ultan with a shield maiden flashed before her. Which one? Did she care? Not really.

"Astrid, Dulca's other wife, is in love with Bjorn," he continued spraying out a mouthful of bath water like a child. "He's besotted."

"What's she like?" Sonas asked.

"Pretty. Young. Possibly not much older than Bjorn, clever, and...why do you want to know about her?"

"She's my husband's other wife. I want to know my rivals."

"There's something else we need to discuss," Ultan said with a frown. "You're another Norse's woman. A jarl's wife. I'll need to know what you want to do when Dulca returns."

"What will Dulca do?" Sonas asked. "You cannot fight him. He's much too...big."

"Agreed." Ultan hiccupped. "And if you divorce him, you'll no longer be a jarl in his absence. He's also not at fault and might become bitter."

"Or...he might agree to me bedding you both?" Sonas said and hid her smirk behind the drying cloth she folded. "If you could have more than one woman, perhaps I could..."

"Is his cock that good?" Ultan asked and sank lower

in the water. "They say he's huge."

"The biggest I've ever seen."

"Stop!"

"Like a hardened, thick snake. Scary."

Ultan laughed. "Is mine enough?" he asked, stood up and revealed an impressive erection.

"Your cock will have to do." Sonas watched as he fisted himself.

"Good," came his reply. "Well, get onto our bed and let me between those sweet thighs." He smoothed excess water from the few hairs on his chest and came for her with lust in his eyes.

"You'll need to be attentive to my needs. Dulca spent all his time pleasuring me." Sonas took off her tunic over her head. "I like things slow and soft to start," she murmured as he crawled up onto the bed beside her. "You're soaking. Don't drip on the new furs."

"Stop ordering me about," Ultan said, "And I know how you like me. I'm going to take you. Rough. For a long time."

"All night?"

"Till dawn."

Chapter Thirty-Six

A Spanking

He hadn't liked the suggestion of her remaining Dulca's woman. He wanted her all to himself; from the salty drop on her top lip to the sweet-tasting juices between her thighs.

As he sank the tip of his aching cock between her wet folds and she wrapped slender legs over his back, he moaned like an animal. He eased in, sensing how tight she was.

He groaned. "Nothing ever feels as good." He sought her mouth and kissed her with an unsatisfiable appetite. Her eyes were half closed in pleasure, and she arched her back and each plowing stroke was even more…more… *Fuck, he was in love. This was more than love, the pleasure was unending… Fuck…By Odin, he would die a happy man if he was taken.*

She ground her pelvis up, scraped his back, and sucked his tongue deep into her mouth. *She drove him berserk. No man could endure her without losing his reason, his mind, his…*

He wanted to last until she was satisfied, but the temptation to release the madness was great. She whimpered enjoyment and urged him deeper. Although he was trying to take more time between re-entering her, his counting and patience waned.

"Don't you dare finish," she said, and bit her bottom lip with a grimace. "Not yet. I need more."

Memories of his shield maiden and Finnegan resurfaced, and he was fit to burst. She sensed his completion was close, for she opened her fist and, with the flat of her palm, spanked him hard across his exposed buttock. The shock stopped him mid-stride, but the sensation sent him one violent last emptying thrust.

He was used to battle wounds, but the slight sting the strike left on his arse left him shuddering in a lasting release inside his woman.

"Dagda!" he panted. "Your god, you summon often. Now, my lovely, I think you need to call on the Christian God for mercy."

****

His tongue licked from her clit to her opening and back again. His scratchy beard caused a slight pain and an oddly pleasant sensation. He then sucked gently on the pulsing nub and sank two fingers inside her.

"Oh, yes… right there," she purred. "Yes."

She gripped his head and forced him into a growing rhythm. "Finger me like you would use your cock."

"If you keep ordering me about, I'll stop what I'm doing," he said. "I'll not take much more of your demands."

"Hmph."

"You gave me a spanking and I think you deserve it more…"

Her face reddened. *Helga slapped her arse once or twice, and both of them had become aroused by the experience.*

"Would you?" she whispered. "But not too hard."

"Show me," he said and turned Sonas onto her belly.

A calloused hand rasped over her trembling buttocks and thighs as he whispered, "Who taught you?"

"I don't know if I want to be hit."

"You're lying," Ultan said and held her hair back to expose her neck. He bit her and felt her arse. "You will tell me who trounced you before." There was a pretend menace in his voice. "I'm going to make you tell me…"

Sonas held her breath and clenched her thighs together over her probing fingers. She waited for the smack and rubbed her clit in anticipation. *This was going to be good…When would he slap again? How harsh? She was wet and willing for him to continue.*

The slap was glorious and surprised her. His large palm connected with skin in a hot flash of intense pleasure. The next was better and flung her downward onto the mattress.

"More."

This time, the sound and sensation was loud and much harsher. Then there was another and another. "Tell me. I'm going to make your pretty arse pink. You'll not want to sit down. I'll make you beg me to fuck you instead, and I won't…until you tell me."

Sonas shook her head and moaned. "I won't need much more. I'm almost there."

He leaned heavily over her back and flicked his hand across her bare buttocks. She roared and nuzzled her face into the pillow while she rubbed between her legs. *She was close. Too close. She was going to come like never before.*

"A good thrashing is what you need," he said and slipped fingers in to find her wetness.

She dripped and heaved back against him, and pushed into her hand. The struggle to reach the summit was almost over.

"You are ready for cock," he said as his hand clipped off her arse, and then beautifully he hit her again and again.

This was all she needed. The powerful sensation rattled through her and lingered like the hot aches in her burning cheeks.

Before she could compose herself, Ultan urged her onto her knees and found the place he needed. The movement of his groin on her sore skin, the noise of flesh on flesh, and the grunts of his interest was bliss. She strained against his riding motion and lost herself in the deep thrusts. Her knees grew tired and were just about to buckle when he came, pumping hotness across the small of her back.

"You never told me what I wanted to know," he said with a sigh and flopped into the furs.

She lay beside him, curling against the chest she loved. "Where would the fun be, then?"

"I'll have to spank you again."

"Oh dear," she said, giggling.

"If you can tell me lies easily, I worry about what else you are keeping from me."

"I warned you the first night you took me to your bed...I'm not the woman you think I am. I told you, I have many secrets."

Chapter Thirty-Seven

A Killing

How many times had he sat and watched her work around a longhouse? He felt as if he always had...like she was a part of him and was always there. He was silly, of course, for he was fighting to be a greater man when she came into his life. She was destined to be close to him and scared him in those early days. There was no way of knowing what magic or spells she cast, and he ran away. Yet, she gave him no reason to mistrust her, and the gods gifted her beauty to him, and he had rejected her. Those who embraced Sonas flourished...Or did they? Helga was forlorn, and Dulca's homeland had been invaded? But these things were far away from where Sonas was. She was a talisman for good luck. When those who loved her were not in her presence, they suffered more than grief. Had Dulca realized, too?

Loki whispered about Sonas, saying she was a bad omen. But Loki was the badness in Ultan's life. Old Finnegan suggested Loki might know more about his father's disappearance. Loki was in Fiordland, and they'd journeyed together to Upvhal while Arden hunted. Helga all but admitted her role in Arden's disappearance. Yet...Loki's whispering brought about all the awful situations. Darkness always lingered where Loki walked.

"The battles were O'Donnell's doing," Oisin said and stoked the fire pit. "There'll be more attacks unless there is a truce."

"Don't look at me," Ultan said. "Ask Sonas of the Flames."

"But she's your woman."

"This is to be decided."

"Don't you take charge?"

Ultan chuckled and recalled the night's activities. "I try to. But in my world, a free woman has the right to make choices, and Sonas is the wife of a jarl. She has greater power than me."

"Doesn't it bother ya?"

"Yes, but the magic surrounding Sonas has brought her good status. In Upvhal she slept with the dogs. Look at her now. I cannot help but admire all she has achieved."

Oisin looked surprised.

"She was a thrall or slave," Ultan said. "She was a princess here. She has proven herself worthy to be a leader again and…"

"A princess? Here?" Oisin scoffed. "Her auld father would enjoy the description of her as a princess. Ha."

"Is she not high born?" Ultan asked.

"I suppose she is. But she's also a pagan, and to her father, she had little value. He couldn't wait to be rid of her."

"And look what happened to him," Ultan mused aloud. "He lost his head. She always swore to get her vengeance and even from far away. She has a great magic. I'm convinced of this. From the moment I took her across the ocean, I knew…Loki knew."

"He's a vicious animal," Oisin said. "Loki stole

away from here and the attacks started. He's like a bad omen."

"What are you two plotting?" Sonas touched Ultan's shoulder. "All is quiet this morning. Foggy and cold. Hopefully, the O'Donnells are licking their wounds and are growing tired of losing their fighting men. I know in other places you have settled with little resistance. I've heard the tales from other traders. Why could this not happen here?"

Ultan rubbed his beard. "Those Norsemen have many ships. They're also kings. And things are not easy for the less wealthy warriors."

His amber mine, and of what other riches were hidden in the earth around his settlement. Perhaps, too, this little stinking hovel had riches Sonas did not know about. The harbor was good, and the stream was passable for boats. The forests were sparse enough for trekking inland, and the farmers were excellent and had cultivated plenty of space for crops in the fertile soil across the marshes of the freshwater lake. For a Norse, there was much here to place roots, and the Celts also saw these advantages, but perhaps even more riches lay under the soil or in the snow-capped mountains in the distance.

"Dulca sent me here on those raids, or should I say he granted me permission, and something drew me farther east from the monks' islands close by," Ultan said. "Dulca said to go to the mainland and see about settling. He's never wrong in his plots to advance his legacy."

"He didn't know about the clans and the infighting." Sonas reached for some bread across the table.

"I think he depended on this fact." Ultan held his

185

woman's hand. "But he thought a pagan princess of their own might join them under a Norse banner. Clever."

"Hmph!"

"Oisin, you don't think I can lead us into something better?" Sonas asked her cousin.

Ultan rubbed her fingers between his own. *Oisin was a cowardly weasel. Why did he stay with her father when the rest had left? Someone should ask him, but in time, the truth usually rose to the surface.*

"I do....," Oisin said.

"Well, tell me why you disrespect me?" Sonas asked. "Explain to me why you snort and chortle at everything I say."

"I don't mean to mock. My problem is you're just a Norse whore, and nothing more."

Ultan seized him by the throat and his muscles tightened. His eyes flashed with anger. His grip cut off the man's air and the vein in his temple throbbed as he squeezed harder. "What did you say? Sonas is your queen, your jarl, and my woman."

He could kill the skinny bag of bones in minutes.

Sonas sat on the bench and ate her bread as if nothing was happening. Oisin made no progress in removing Ultan's strangle-hold. Having a man's fate in his hands was quite enjoyable, and exhausting. He was just about to ask Sonas for her decision about what to do when Oisin went limp under him. When Ultan looked down, Sonas removed her sword from the man's abdomen. Pools of blood soaked out.

"Dulca told me to use my sword on any man who annoyed me," she said with a coldness Ultan had not seen before. "He also showed me the quickest and quietest way to puncture a man's liver and slice his innards. And I've been wanting to slice him open for a long time."

There was a new kind of awe in Ultan's heart for this woman, and yet his heart beat a few times before he stopped the niggle of doubt in his heart. *Sonas would never harm him. But just in case, he would give her no reason to.*

Chapter Thirty-Eight

An Ending

Sonas shook (only slightly) from the murder. The tremble came from the sight of the blood and a lack of expected remorse. *A whore gave her body to others to use for their pleasure, and really, she was one. Her actions were for survival, a way to achieve something, and she always lusted after the people involved. Was her whoring something to be ashamed of? Ultan had been quiet since she spoke, eyeing her suspiciously and possibly wondering what happened to the meek slave he took to his bed. Yes, where had she gone?*

The messenger from O'Donnell did not stay long. His face was ashen, and his voice trembled. "Our Lord O'Donnell is badly injured from battle and until he recovers, there will be no discussions."

"Is he gravely ill?" Ultan asked with hope. "Perhaps your curse is working, my love?"

Sonas grinned and patted Gruff's furry head. Her seat at the head of the fire pit was warm and gave her resolve. Finnegan stood to her right, and he whittled a small carving and pretended he was not interested or listening. The servant scuttled out like a scalded cat, and Finnegan chuckled. Ultan walked around menacingly. Gruff was nervous, but this gave Sonas a chance to admire her fine man.

Tall, handsome, muscular, and an excellent fighter. She adored him and worked hard at hiding the fact. This was good, for he would work hard to keep her interest. He liked her unpredictability. Helga taught her the element of seduction. "Treat men mean," *she'd said. Sonas had admired Helga's mind and how her actions caused shock. This drew Sonas to Helga, and she stood apart from all the other women. She was strong, unafraid, and independent.*

"Sit down, Ultan the Fearless," Sonas ordered. "My dog does not trust you."

"I don't trust the mutt either."

"But you respect me?" she asked. *Suddenly, she wanted him to tell her of his love in front of the people in her longhouse.* "You love me? You'll stay here and help me rule?"

Ultan opened his mouth and looked around.

Sonas waited, watching Ultan. One by one conversations around her died down. Even Gruff stopped gnawing on a bone as if he, too, waited for Ultan to answer. *When she had cast her spells, she asked for revenge for his abandoning her, and she prayed he would lose his soul, his body, and his mind...to her. Now, the tables had turned. Ultan the Fearless craved and needed her. Needed Sonas of the Flames. He would agree. If he did not...could she forgive him?*

****

Ultan could not speak. His mind was muddled like snakes in a pit. *What was Sonas asking him? Apart from when they humped, Sonas never requested anything from him. Yet in front of many strangers (and Finnegan) she put him under pressure to reveal his innermost thoughts. He rarely allowed a woman to back him into a corner.*

What was he going to do? She had just run a man through with her blade for telling her something she did not like. A man would need to be careful, but he had already decided to forgo whatever seat he might hold in Upvhal for her. Saying the words out loud would be difficult because he did not know her decision about Dulca. What would the Beast think of their union? Dulca was not here to claim her.

His Norse heart belonged to Sonas, and his cock had never been happier…She should know, but she always found a way to shock him and pull him off balance. Perhaps, too, she needed him to commit in front of witnesses and for her peace of mind. Maybe she was not as sure of herself as she would have him believe.

"I always knew those eyes of yours were trouble." His voice was loud, like he was beginning a story. "I love and adore you, my Celtic princess, Sonas of the Flames. My sacrifice will be to relinquish whatever power I may have in Upvhal to be by your side. Is this what you need to know? However, I also have a question for you. What do you feel about me? You already have a husband. Do you respect and love me?"

She looked uncertain, and he dug his nails into his palm. *Would she make him look foolish? She could easily take what remaining power he had and fling all into the fire. When they fucked, she loved him…Wasn't this passion for him alone? She slept with Helga, but there was no love between them. And she admired Dulca, but theirs was not true love. She cared for him. Only him. He was certain…*

He searched her expression for clues to her answer, but her beauty was calm.

****

Sonas stood in front of her fearless warrior. When she looked deep into his eyes, she saw the kind eyes from their first meeting in Upvhal.

"The gods had a purpose for us both when they brought us together," she said. "They've shown us we should not be apart. Jarl Dulca, and everyone else, knows you are my only love. And I accept the sacrifice you'll make for me. I'll give gratitude to you and the gods for this. I only ask you to be always true to me, Ultan the Fearless, and I'll always be true to you. Forever."

His broad shoulders loomed large as his handsome smile leaned down to meet her eager lips.

To the whoops and Finnegan's whistles, Sonas of the Flames kissed her Norse warrior.

A word about the author...

Penny Best is the pen name of a best-selling writer who lives on the beautiful Inishowen peninsula in the northwest of Ireland. In true romantic style, this is where she fell in love, rescued puppies, and made a home. sharonthompson.substack.com